The Sickness

Even the book morphs!
Flip the pages
and check it out!

Look for other **ANIMORPHS** titles by K.A. Applegate:

ANIMORPHS®

The Sickness

K.A. Applegate

AN
APPLE
PAPERBACK

SCHOLASTIC INC.
New York Toronto London Auckland Sydney
Mexico City New Delhi Hong Kong

ISBN 0-590-76262-1

12 11 10 9 8 7 6 5 4 3 2 1   9/9 0 1 2 3 4/0

Printed in the U.S.A.   40

First Scholastic printing, May 1999

The author wishes to thank Melinda Metz for her
help in preparing this manuscript.

For Michael and Jake

The Sickness

CHAPTER 1

My name is Cassie.

I wish I could tell you my whole name. Because that would mean I was a nice, normal girl. But I'm not either one. Not nice. Not normal.

Okay, my friends think I'm nice. Marco is always calling me a tree-hugger. And even though I don't actually hug trees, I do care about them. Which makes me nice, right? A girl who cares about trees can't be anything but nice.

Unless that girl has also ripped a living creature's throat out with her bare teeth. Which I have.

I was in wolf morph, deep in battle. Seven Hork-Bajir against six of us. Jake gave the order to retreat. And either right before he said it, or

1

right after, I yanked the throat out of the Hork-Bajir I was fighting.

I hope it was right before. I hope that I didn't go in for the kill when I could have just run. But I'm not sure.

That's why I don't think I qualify as nice. You've probably already gotten a clue why I don't qualify as normal.

Here's the short version: An Andalite prince named Elfangor gave the power to morph to me and four of my friends. He knew he was about to die, and he didn't want to leave Earth defenseless against the Yeerk invasion.

He showed us a small blue box. We pressed our hands against it. And we were changed.

This morphing cube was lost for a while. Now we have it again. We've used it once, to add an Animorph to our group.

Then we had to subtract that new Animorph. And we've kept the blue box hidden ever since.

Since that night in the construction site, since that change, the five of us, plus Elfangor's younger brother, have been fighting the Yeerks.

Yeerks are parasites. A Yeerk enters a host through the ear canal, flattens itself out on the brain, and takes over completely. The host creature can't scratch an itch unless the Yeerk wants it to. We call a being who has been taken over that way a Controller.

You must be thinking the Yeerks are pure evil. But let me tell you what it's like to be a Yeerk who isn't in a host. Yeerks are basically gray slugs. No hands, no legs, no eyes, no ears.

If a Yeerk wants to be free, free to really move, free to see the beauty of the world around it, free to hear music or even the sound of rain on leaves, if a Yeerk wants that, it has to have a host. If a Yeerk wants to be free, it has to make another living creature a slave.

Not an easy choice, is it?

I know something about hard choices. I've made a lot of them since I became an Animorph. And one of the hardest was whether I wanted to be an Animorph at all. Because I know that when — if — this whole thing is over, it may be too late for me to be either nice or normal ever again.

Like I said, I know something about hard choices.

"So, Cassie, here's your choice. If you were on a desert island, who would you want to be with you — Baby Spice or Marco?" Rachel asked as we sat down at our usual lunch table.

"Huh?" What else could I say to that question?

"It's the desert island game," Rachel answered. "You pick two annoying people. Then you have to choose which of them you'd rather be on a desert island with."

3

I glanced across the cafeteria at Marco. He and Jake were sitting at a table by the windows.

"Marco is not —" I began.

Rachel grabbed me by the arm. "Hey, shush. Listen to Allison and Brittany," she whispered.

I pulled my yogurt from my backpack and tried to eavesdrop without looking like I was eavesdropping. Allison and Brittany were sitting at the other end of our table.

"Maybe I should ask him to the dance," Allison said.

This is what Rachel wanted me to hear?

"Do it," Brittany urged. "Jake has gotten so cute."

Wait. Did she say *Jake*? *The* Jake? Or some other Jake?

I shot a glance at Brittany and Allison. They both stared over at Jake. As in Jake, the leader of the Animorphs. As in *my* Jake.

Now you're probably picturing us walking around school hand-in-hand, maybe kissing by the lockers before class. But it's not like that. It's more an inside kind of thing. We've only kissed one time. Although I would like it to happen again.

But most people at school don't have a clue we're together. Obviously.

"Hey, Allison. Hey, listen up." Allison looked

over and Rachel shook her head slowly. "Uh-uh. Don't even think about it. Jake's with Cassie."

My face got hot as both Brittany and Allison started checking me out. I'm not beautiful like Rachel. And I admit I sometimes have a little bird poop on my jeans. I spend a lot of time helping my dad take care of the animals at the Wildlife Rehabilitation Center he has out in our barn, and birds, being birds, will poop.

But that stuff doesn't matter to Jake. I know how he feels about me.

Allison tossed her long red ponytail over her shoulder. "It doesn't *look* like Cassie and Jake are together," she told Rachel. "He's sitting over there. She's here. There, here. Waaayyy over there, as opposed to right here."

"Yeah," Brittany chimed in. "Has Jake even asked her to the dance?"

They didn't even ask *me* their questions. They acted like I was invisible. I'm used to that. Rachel is one of these people who seem to go through life with a spotlight focused on them at all times.

"The dance? Of course he asked her to the dance," Rachel said.

Then she stood up and grabbed my yogurt in one hand and my backpack in the other. "Allison, Brittany, we, Cassie and I, are going over there. Waaayyy over there."

Rachel marched across the cafeteria toward Marco and Jake. I had no choice but to follow.

"You and my cousin make me want to hurl," she said over her shoulder. "Jake can face death every day, but he can't manage to ask a girl to a dance. And you're no better."

"Me? What am I supposed to do?" I protested.

"Duh. Even Allison the Airhead knows," Rachel said.

Rachel sat down next to Marco. She put my yogurt down next to Jake. I took the hint and sat next to him.

"We are all going to the dance Thursday night," Rachel informed Jake. "And you are taking Cassie."

Jake choked on his macaroni and beef. Marco started banging him on the back.

"So, Rachel, I guess that means you need a date, too, huh?" Marco said. "I could make time in my busy schedule."

"Look at that! A flying pig!" Rachel exclaimed. Then, "Oh, sorry, my mistake. I thought for a minute I saw a flying pig. But I didn't. And that's the only time I would go out with you."

Jake was recovering. His face was red. I waited for him to tell them we wouldn't be going to the dance. I thought he'd say that we had to

spend that night doing some kind of Yeerk sur-
veillance or something.

But Jake just smiled at me. "We *could* use a
night doing something nice and normal."

"Oh, man," Marco moaned.

"What?"

"Every time we try to do something nice and
normal it ends up turning out nasty and weird,"
he said. "Every single time."

CHAPTER 2

The dance.

Picture loud music. Picture chips and dip and a bowl of trail mix. Picture the lights low, the decorations limp, the teachers standing outside the rest rooms discussing whether there would be a teachers' strike.

Picture guys mostly with guys, girls mostly with girls. But with lots of eye contact.

Not my kind of place, really. Rachel had forced me to wear a dress. She had dragged me through the mall, dressing me up like her own personal Barbie doll.

I had on shoes I could never run in. I was even wearing makeup.

I felt like the largest, most obvious dweeb in the history of dweebs.

"Ax-man, someone is checking you out," Marco said.

I wasn't surprised that Ax was getting some attention. His human morph is cute. More pretty than cute, really.

"No way. She's looking at *me*," Tobias said. He shot a quick look at Rachel to see how she liked the idea of another girl giving him the eye.

"Uh-huh. Maybe after the dance you could take her back to your tree," Rachel said, batting her eyes at Tobias.

Tobias laughed. "Hey, the chicks go wild for the feathers, bay-beee." He laughed again. "Sorry. Ax had Austin Powers on his TV last night."

I looked at Allison. Marco was right. She *was* staring at Ax. I guess she figured if she couldn't have Jake, she'd go for the cute new boy.

Not that Tobias isn't cute. And he might as well be a new boy. He went to our school for a while, back when he was human. Back before he was trapped in his red-tailed hawk morph.

Now no one seemed to recognize him. But, then, he's totally different from the kid bullies used to pick on. He doesn't project those I'm-helpless-so-come-and-terrorize-me vibes at all anymore.

Partly that comes from living a life where even the good times are dangerous. Partly it's that he's sort of forgotten how to express emotions with his face. Smiling when he's happy just isn't natural to him anymore, because hawks don't smile. Now when people look at Tobias, they notice the strangeness of his blank face, not the face itself. Even when he laughs he doesn't really smile.

"Checking me out? What does that mean?" Ax asked.

"It means that girl over there is warm for your form," Marco told him. "It means she wants your body."

Ax started to look a little nervous. "My bod-deee? Body, body, bawd-eee?"

Ax normally does not have a mouth. In human morph, with a mouth, Ax can be . . . unusual.

"She's making her move," Marco told Ax. "Although if you want to get rid of her just try saying 'bod-eee' like that a few times."

"Buh-dee. B-dee," Ax said, continuing to play with the sound.

Of course if Allison knew what Ax really looks like, she'd run screaming in the other direction.

Ax's Andalite body is strange. Strange and beautiful and intimidating, too. Picture this: a blue-and-tan deer-like body, a giant scorpion tail, a pair of small arms, a humanoid head with no mouth, and two extra eyeballs mounted on stalks.

Allison stopped in front of Ax. She smiled and tossed her red hair around.

"Hi. I wanted to know if you, you know, want to dance?" Allison said.

Ax nodded. "I would like to shuffle my artificial hooves to the music with you. But you cannot have my body. My bod. Dee. My bo. Dee."

Allison backed away. "Ah. Oh. You know what? I hear my friend calling me," she said. Then bolted.

A wild burst of laughter escaped my mouth. I couldn't help myself. The expression on Allison's face —

"Bo. Dee," Ax repeated. "I enjoy the way my tongue hits the front of my mouth when I say that. Dee. Oh! Food! Do they possess the delightful flavors of grease, salt, and sugar here?"

Ax also likes to use his mouth to eat. To a dangerous extent.

Sometimes when I watch Ax experiencing the sense of taste I find myself thinking about the Yeerks. When they enter a host they get hit with thousands of new sensations.

I can hardly wrap my mind around what it must feel like. I have to narrow it down for myself. I'll pick one thing, like color. Then I'll close my eyes and try to imagine I have never seen any color of any kind.

When I open my eyes the array of colors

11

around me makes me dizzy. And color is only one part of sight. And sight is only one of the new senses Yeerks experience in a host.

I didn't bother telling my friends what I was thinking about. None of them are all that interested in considering the joys a Yeerk can find in a host. Not that I blame them.

Yeerks are the enemy. It's easier for us to do our job if we see them as evil. Pure evil.

I shook my head and told myself that a dance wasn't the time to get all philosophical. Especially my first real kind of date with Jake. A date involving an actual dress. And makeup. I tuned back in to the conversation.

"Baby Spice or Oprah?" Marco was saying, looking thoughtfully at Rachel.

"What do you have against Oprah?"

"She's on my list of 'people I've heard way too much about.'"

"You have an actual list?" Tobias asked skeptically.

I smiled. It was just dumb, normal, pointless conversation. It was nice to be normal sometimes.

Jake must have felt the same way. Our eyes met. "Want to dance?"

"I'm not very good," I said.

"I dance like a lumberjack," Jake said.

"Like a lumberjack who's just chopped off one of his own legs," Marco interjected helpfully. "Like a one-legged lumberjack whose remaining leg is a tree stump and —"

Jake grabbed my hand and pulled me out onto the dance floor. The dance floor formerly known as the basketball court. And then I was dancing. With Jake.

I gave a little twirl of happiness. Is it horrible to admit that I hoped everyone was watching? Especially Allison?

Even if it's horrible, it's true. I liked the idea of everyone knowing that I, Cassie of the some-times-bird-pooped jeans, was with Jake.

Jake smiled at me. He has a great smile, even though it always looks a little strange on his face. Just because he's usually so intense, making life-and-death decisions for us all. Making more hard choices than I ever have to make.

I smiled back, and gave another twirl. I spotted Ax, Marco, Rachel, and Tobias dancing in a group nearby. I hoped that Rachel and Tobias got a chance to break away and have a dance by themselves.

I tried to catch Rachel's eye. I thought maybe I could give her some kind of signal that she and Tobias shouldn't spend the whole night hanging with Ax and Marco.

But Rachel's gaze was locked on Ax. As I watched, an expression of amazed horror crossed her face.

What was wrong? I jerked my eyes to Ax, and felt my own face twist into an expression that mirrored Rachel's.

Ax's head! A lump on the top of Ax's head was throbbing to the music.

"We have a problem," I whispered to Jake.

CHAPTER 3

Jake and I shoved our way through the mass of bopping, spinning, shaking bodies. By the time we got to the group, Marco had his flannel shirt off. He started to fold the shirt into a bandana just as —

Boing!

Ax's eye stalk burst out of the lump.

I did a quick scan of the gym. Had anyone seen? No. Everyone was busy dancing. Or hoping someone would ask them to dance. Or psyching themselves up to ask someone to dance.

Rachel grabbed the shirt out of Marco's hands and wrapped it around Ax's head.

And here's the thing about Rachel, even in a crisis: The bandana actually looked good.

15

"Ax, you're starting to demorph. You've got to stop," Jake told him.

Ax giggled. "Demorph. Dee, dee. That is a very pleasant mouth sound. Dee!"

"He's delirious," I said. I felt the adrenaline start to pump through my body. This was a very bad situation here.

"Another dee," Ax said happily, swaying.

I heard a soft shushing sound. And a patch of blue fur sprouted on Ax's neck.

"Equipment room should be empty," Jake said. "To the right of the bleachers. Far side. Move, move, move!"

We formed a circle around Ax and headed across the dark, noisy gym as fast as we could.

We reached the equipment-room door. I grabbed the doorknob. Turned it.

Locked.

"Out the guys' locker-room windows," Marco said.

"Two teachers always supervising in there," Jake reminded him.

"Not in the girls'," Rachel told him.

"Go straight behind the punch table. The line in front will give us some cover," Jake ordered.

"You're telling me there's no teachers monitoring the girls' room?" Marco demanded. "That is so unfair!"

We squeezed between the punch table and the wall, all of us keeping one hand on Ax.

"We'll meet up in the parking lot," Jake said when we reached the locker room. He, Marco, and Tobias let go of Ax and turned toward the main exit.

I jerked open the door. And Brittany and Allison walked out in a cloud of Love's Baby Soft perfume.

"She wants my body! BDEEE! BDEEE!" Ax screeched in terror. He broke away from me and Rachel and bolted for the main exit.

"He's heading toward Chapman and Mr. Tidwell," Rachel cried.

Vice Principal Chapman. A known Controller.

And Mr. Tidwell. The strictest teacher in the school.

We all tore after Ax. We caught up to him just as Chapman grabbed him by the arm.

Ax's flannel-shirt turban had gotten loose during his dash across the gym. One shake of his head could send the shirt fluttering to the floor.

Giving Chapman a good look at Ax's eye stalk. A fatal look.

"He's obviously been drinking," Mr. Tidwell said. "I know this boy. I'll call his parents."

Before Chapman could answer, Mr. Tidwell

17

marched Ax out of the gym and into the hallway. We started after them.

Chapman blocked us. "No one is allowed outside the gym until the dance is over unless a parent gives permission."

"We're his friends. We have his medication," I blurted. A delirious Ax alone with Mr. Tidwell — that couldn't happen.

Chapman studied us for a moment.

"Two minutes," he said. He stepped aside and we slammed through the door.

We acted without hesitation. Rachel and Marco squeezed between Ax and Mr. Tidwell. Jake, Tobias, and I pulled Ax down the hall to the drinking fountain and shoved his head down. We huddled close, trying to block Mr. Tidwell's view with our bodies.

I took a quick glance at Mr. Tidwell. How were Rachel and Marco doing?

They stood shoulder-to-shoulder in front of Mr. Tidwell, keeping some hallway between him and Ax. At least for now.

"He's from out of town," I heard Rachel say as I turned back to Ax. "Jake knows what to do."

"He takes special pills," Marco added desperately. "For narcolepsy. Or epilepsy. Some kind of epsy."

"In a few minutes he'll be fine," Rachel promised.

I shot another look their way. Mr. Tidwell hadn't budged. He was staring straight toward Ax.

I leaned even closer to Ax and whispered in his ear. "Ax, can you get your human morph all the way back? At least until we make it outside?"

Ax didn't answer. His lips were melting together.

"Mr. Tidwell! Some guys in the bathroom have cherry bombs. They're going to blow the lids off all the toilets!" Marco yelled. "It'll be a toilet massacre!"

Tidwell still hadn't taken a step back toward the gym. But Rachel and Marco had kept him from moving toward us. So far.

Two legs shot out of Ax's chest.

KA-BANG. KA-BANG. The hooves slammed against the tile wall over the drinking fountain.

Chinkle, plop, chinkle. Tile and plaster rained down onto the metal fountain.

Tidwell might not have seen that. But he had to have heard it.

"See?" Marco yelled. "Cherry bombs everywhere!"

Shloop. Shloop. Ax's legs sucked back into his chest.

P-p-pop. His lips separated.

Ax looked like a regular kid again. "The medicine is kicking in," I called. I shot a frantic glance at Mr. Tidwell.

"We should get him home," Jake said loudly. Then he lowered his voice. "Now we walk him past Tidwell and hope Ax can keep it together until we get outside."

Jake started down the hall first. Tobias and I each took one of Ax's arms and fell in behind.

It was going to work. Ax wasn't babbling or demorphing. Mr. Tidwell wasn't yelling for our parents' phone numbers.

In another three steps, we'd reach him. Then in two more steps we'd be past him.

One. Two.

Riiiip.

I did not like that sound. I did not like it at all.

I looked over my shoulder just in time to see Ax's giant scorpion tail tear through his pants, swing to the left — and knock Mr. Tidwell on his butt.

CHAPTER 4

I rushed over to Mr. Tidwell and helped him up.

"Are you okay?" I asked. At least Ax caught him with the side of the blade. Otherwise Mr. Tidwell's head might be staring up from the floor at his own body.

Mr. Tidwell didn't answer. He just took me by the elbow and led me down the hall away from the others.

What was he doing? What did he want with me? The adrenaline had started pumping back in the gym. Now I could practically feel it slamming through my veins.

I shot a look over my shoulder. Marco and To-

21

bias huddled around Ax. Jake was holding Rachel back from going after us. "Don't say anything," he mouthed to me.

I knew what was going through Jake's mind. It was going through mine, as well: Tidwell could not know. Could not. No matter the price.

"We really should get our friend —" I began when Mr. Tidwell pulled me to a stop.

"Don't. I know your friend is an Andalite," he told me, his voice calm and matter-of-fact.

My mouth went dry. My throat, too. Just became a total desert. I wanted to tell Mr. Tidwell that I had no idea what he was talking about. But I couldn't get out a word.

"I also know who you are and what you are. All of you," Mr. Tidwell continued.

Sweat popped out on my hands, under my arms, and down the center of my back. It was like all the moisture from my mouth and throat had migrated. Migrated and multiplied.

Mr. Tidwell was a Controller. No question about that. And that meant he could not walk away. Could not live to hurt us, to destroy us.

I prepared to morph.

I heard Ax's hooves slam into the wall again. But I didn't take my eyes off Mr. Tidwell.

He looked so ordinary. Thinning gray-brown hair. A little bit of a paunch. Wire-rim glasses. Medium-blue eyes.

But that's the thing with Controllers: They look like anyone. They *are* anyone.

"I am Illim. I control Mr. Tidwell. We are both part of the Yeerk peace movement. We have a message for you from Aftran Nine Four Two," he continued.

I turned and gave Jake an I'm-okay-give-me-a-minute signal. I needed to hear what Mr. Tidwell had to say.

He knew Aftran. Maybe that meant Mr. Tidwell was a friend, too. Make that Illim, the Yeerk inside Mr. Tidwell's head, because that's really who I was talking to. I felt the muscles in my shoulders relax the tiniest bit.

Aftran is the Yeerk who made me think about Yeerks in a different way. Aftran made me realize that Yeerks are individuals, no two alike. She forced me to accept that all Yeerks are not our enemies.

The night I ripped the throat out of the Hork-Bajir, I also killed Aftran's brother. Aftran's brother was the Yeerk controlling the Hork-Bajir.

Aftran, in the body of Karen, her little girl host, had tracked me down, planning to turn me over to Visser Three.

Long story short: I saved her life. She saved my life. And then Aftran willingly returned to life as a blind, helpless, sluglike creature. She sacrificed her freedom to free Karen.

"Dee! Buh-DEE!" Ax bellowed, jerking me out of my thoughts.

I cleared my throat. "What message?"

"Aftran has been taken by Yeerk security," he answered.

"When?" I demanded. "Is she okay? What has she told them? Why didn't you find me sooner?"

Mr. Tidwell held up both hands. "Aftran is unharmed, for now. She hasn't been questioned yet," he told me. "Visser Three wants to handle the interrogation personally."

A cold lump formed in my stomach. Interrogation by Visser Three meant torture. I was sure Aftran would hold out as long as she could. But she would end up telling the Visser everything she knew.

Which was everything I knew. Aftran had been inside my head. She had unlocked all my memories. She knew all there was to know about the Animorphs.

"When?" I asked. I wrapped my arms around myself.

I caught a flash of movement out of the corner of my eye. Ax's legs were slamming out of his chest and getting sucked back in. Over and over.

"The interrogation will be held in the next few days," Mr. Tidwell answered. "The Visser is attending a reinduction seminar on the Blade ship."

So we had a little time. We could stop this.

Mr. Tidwell's watery blue eyes searched my face. "I'm sure you understand that Aftran could destroy the Yeerk peace movement. And you."

I nodded. "Where is she being held?"

Mr. Tidwell swallowed hard. "Aftran is imprisoned in the Yeerk pool. We need your help getting her out."

The Yeerk pool. The perfect place for an ambush.

I told myself to start acting smart. I couldn't believe whatever Mr. Tidwell said just because he used Aftran's name.

"How do we know this isn't a trap?" I asked, searching Mr. Tidwell's face. "How do we know we can trust you?"

"If you couldn't trust me, you'd be dead right now," he answered. He glanced at the gym door. "If I don't go back in, Chapman will come looking for us. I'll be in touch. Get the Andalite out of here."

Mr. Tidwell hurried back into the gym. I hurried back over to Ax and the others.

"Are we just going to let Tidwell walk back in there?" Rachel demanded. "After what he saw?"

"He's with the Yeerk peace movement," I said.

"Yeah, that's where they say please before they shove their slimy bodies into your ear and

25

take control of your brain," Marco spat out. "What are you, crazy?"

"He saved us from Chapman tonight," I protested.

"So what?"

"Shut up!" Tobias snapped, in a totally un-Tobias way. "All I care about right now is getting Ax home."

"He's right. Let's move," Jake said.

I wrapped my arm around Ax's shoulders and helped Tobias lead him outside.

I didn't like the way Ax was looking. He was completely back in his human morph. But a gooey green-yellow pus was gluing his eyelashes together. And his lips were chapped, like when you have a high fever.

"How are you doing, Ax?" I asked.

"I am dee-dee-dee-lirious!" he cried.

CHAPTER 5

As soon as we got outside the school, I managed to talk Ax through the demorph into his Andalite body. Once he was back in his own form, he stayed there. Big relief.

Tobias demorphed, too. He flew overhead and told us which streets to use to avoid the most people. And where to hide Ax when we were close to getting caught. We made it back to the barn, but it was not a fun trip.

"Put him in the last stall," I instructed. "Marco, fill the trough with water. Rachel, get him a blanket from the pile by the door. Jake, go to my house and get the thermometer from the bathroom; I can't use the veterinary equipment. I

27

need the one you can use in your ear. Don't worry about my parents. Out."

I glanced up and saw all three of them staring at me. It's true that I'm not usually the one barking the orders. But I'm the one who knows about taking care of sick animals. Not that Ax is an animal, exactly.

"I feel like I'm on *ER*," Marco said as he headed toward the hose. "I've definitely got a Noah Wyle kind of thing happening."

<Anything I should do?> Tobias asked from his perch in the rafters.

"Just keep a lookout," I answered.

<You got it,> Tobias said.

Rachel hurried over and handed a blanket to me. I spread it over Ax's back and shoulders. I could feel tiny tremors racing through him.

"So are you finally going to tell us what Tidwell said or what?" Marco asked as he filled the trough. "I mean, if some Hork-Bajir are going to burst in the door any second I might want to bake a cake or something."

"Ax is sick, Marco. We have to deal with that first," I answered.

"If Tidwell talks, Ax is going to be worse than sick. He's going to be dead. We all are!" Rachel spat out. "Cassie, what did you say to him? What did he say to you?"

I ignored her. Had to. She spun away and started pacing back and forth in front of the stall.

"Can you tell me what's wrong with you, Ax?" I asked. "Have you ever felt like this before?"

<*Yamphut*,> he mumbled.

"What's that?" I asked.

I needed Ax to tell me what to do to cure him. My parents are both vets. We probably have the best animal medicine library for miles. But there was nothing in any of those books about the care and feeding of an alien.

"Come on, Ax," I said, my voice a little sharper. "What's *yamphut*?"

<It's a . . .> Ax's thought-speak faded.

<Ax, come on. Stay with us,> Tobias said.

"Let's try giving him a little water," I said. "Help me stick one of his hooves in, okay, Marco?" I asked.

Marco topped off the trough and turned off the hose. Then we gently lifted Ax's right front leg and then placed his hoof into the water.

Ax swayed, and I braced my shoulder against his side, letting him lean on me while he absorbed the water. I could feel him heaving against me as he pulled in ragged breaths.

"That's enough," I said when Ax's hoof had been submerged about half a minute.

Marco and I pulled his hoof out of the trough.

29

Rachel grabbed another blanket and tossed it to Marco so he could dry Ax off. I stayed close in case he got wobbly again.

"Okay, Ax. Try and focus. Tell us what *yamphut* is," I said, speaking slowly and clearly.

<Disease,> Ax answered. <Disease organisms collecting in my *Tria* gland.>

Jake rushed back into the barn. "Got the thermometer." He slapped it into my hand scrubnurse style. Then he sat down and leaned against the side of the stall.

I slid the thermometer into Ax's ear and waited for it to beep. When it did, I pulled it out and checked the reading. "Ninety-five point five," I told the others.

"I was sure he had a fever," Rachel said.

"He might," I told Rachel. "But we don't know. Because we don't know what normal Andalite temperature is!"

"Ax? Can you tell us?" Rachel asked him.

<Ninety-one point three,> Ax gasped. <Of your degrees,> he added.

"Ax, they are everyone's degrees, not our degrees," Marco started to argue. Then he stopped.

About four degrees above normal. I wasn't liking this. I knew a few ways to try and break a fever. But I didn't know what effect they would have on an Andalite.

What if something I did made him worse?

"Tell us more about the *Tria* gland," I said.

<*Tria* gland keeps disease organisms away from rest of body,> Ax answered.

<That's good, right?> Tobias asked.

It sounded good. Maybe Ax's body would heal itself.

<But if it bursts. Bad. Disease organisms get loose,> Ax choked out.

"How can we stop it from bursting?" Jake demanded.

Ax locked all four of his eyes on me. He took my hand and gave my fingers a weak squeeze. His skin felt cold and slick with perspiration.

<You must take it out. Or I will die,> he whispered.

His main eyes closed. His stalk eyes drooped. <When temperature goes back to normal . . . *Tria* gland out. Or disease organisms kill.>

"Okay. Okay, yeah. Where is the *Tria* gland?" I asked.

<Tired.>

"I know you're tired. And you can go to sleep soon. But first you have to tell me where the *Tria* gland is," I insisted. "Now, Ax!"

<My head,> Ax answered.

I felt the blood drain from my face. Instinc-

31

tively, I turned to Jake. He was staring at Ax as if he couldn't believe what he'd just heard.

The silence stretched.

"I'm no brain surgeon," Marco finally said. "But it sounds to me like we're talking brain surgery here."

CHAPTER 6

Brain surgery. Images of blood, and scalpels, and delicate tissue. I didn't know if we could do it. But if we didn't, Ax would die.

"Let's move to the other side of the barn," I said. "I want Ax to get some rest."

That was true. But I also didn't want Ax to hear us start to freak, which I knew was about to happen.

"Good idea," Jake said. He pushed himself to his feet and started across the barn, Marco and Rachel following.

I slowly pulled my hand free of Ax's, my fingers slick with his sweat. "I'll be back in a little while," I whispered. "Bless your baby bones."

The words just slipped out of my mouth. It's

what my mom always says to me when I'm sick. Poor Ax. He must really miss his mother right now. At least when I'm not feeling well, I always like my mom making a fuss over me.

And Ax was definitely not feeling well.

I hurried over to the others and sat down on a bale of hay next to Rachel. I was tired.

"Okay, so we kidnap a doctor and get him to do the surgery on Ax," Rachel burst out.

"And then what?" I asked.

She didn't answer. The answer was unacceptable. The only doctor we could trust with our secret was a doctor who quickly became dead.

"I'm going to take his temperature every hour," I said. "We need to know when it drops down to ninety-one point three."

"And then what?" Rachel demanded, echoing my question.

"Then we get to play a live version of Operation. Except if we make a mistake, Ax's nose doesn't light up, his *Tria* gland explodes," Marco answered, his voice flat.

<That's supposed to be funny?> Tobias demanded.

"Yeah. And you want another laugh?" Marco shot back, angry. "Tidwell saw Ax go Andalite tonight!"

"We need to hear what Tidwell said," Jake

told me. He scrubbed his face with his hands. His drawn, pale face.

I pulled in a deep breath. "Mr. Tidwell is part of the peace movement," I began. "The Yeerk inside him, Illim, had a message for me from Aftran. She's been captured. Sunday night Visser Three plans to interrogate her. Illim wants us to rescue her."

"No way. It's a trap," Marco interrupted.

"If the Yeerks already know who we are why bother with a trap? Why not just come to our houses and kill us?"

We both turned to Jake. He rubbed his face again. "Coming to our houses would be messy. Attract attention. Getting us all to the Yeerk pool is a decent strategy."

"Probably it is a trap, but we still have to go," Rachel said. "Because if Tidwell or Illim or whoever is telling the truth, we're dead meat. Aftran will crack when the Visser interrogates her, and she knows everything about us. *Everything.* Right, Cassie?" she said acidly, looking angrily at me.

I met her gaze without blinking. My voice was steady. "That's right," I answered.

I wasn't going to pretend that we wouldn't be in this situation if it wasn't for me.

Marco had been about to kill Aftran. Which meant killing Karen, too. I let Aftran into my own head to get her out of Karen's body.

To save the life of a person I didn't even know, I risked the lives of my friends. I'm not all noble and wonderful. I did it because I was a coward. I couldn't take the life of that little girl — or let Marco do it for me — even though I knew that by letting her live a whole planetful of people might die. Or worse, become infested by Yeerks.

I risked all those lives on a pathetic little wish. A wish that together Aftran and I could make the first step toward peace between Yeerks and humans.

My wish came true. Aftran didn't turn me over to Visser Three. She didn't use the information she found stored in my brain against me and the others. Instead she chose to live without a host. Blind and almost immobile.

My choice turned out to be the right one.

Or had it?

"Rachel's right. We have to go in," Jake decided. "Tonight. If it's a trap, they won't be expecting us this soon, since Illim told us the Visser will be gone until Sunday."

<What about Ax?> Tobias asked.

"That's another reason to go in tonight," I said. "We get back before Ax hits his crisis."

"We can't leave him in the barn," Jake pointed out. "Cassie's dad comes in here all the time."

<Maybe we could fix up some kind of extra shelter around his scoop,> Tobias suggested.

I shook my head. "Too damp in that field," I said.

"Erek," Marco said. "The Chee owe us."

"Good idea, Marco," Jake said. "Go. Now."

CHAPTER 7

Marco morphed and took to the air. The rest of us watched Ax sweat and tremble.

"The Yeerks have probably figured out how we got in last time," Rachel said. "We need a new way in if we don't want to get ambushed."

"Maybe it would help if we go over everything we know about the Yeerk pool's security systems," I suggested. "We know there's the Gleet BioFilter, and —"

<Hunter-killer robots,> Tobias added.

"It was never exactly easy," Jake said. "But it's harder, now."

"There has to be a way," Rachel said.

We went over everything we knew and came up blank. And Ax still trembled.

I checked my watch. Time was running out. My parents would be home soon. First thing my dad would do was come to the barn.

<Here come Erek and Marco,> Tobias announced at last.

I glanced out the barn door. Erek and Marco, walking side by side, fast. If you saw Erek you'd think he was just a normal kid. He looks kind of like Jake, actually, only a little shorter.

But Erek's an android. Part of a race called the Chee. And what you see when you look at him, that's just a hologram. Under the hologram Erek looks a little like a robot dog walking on its hind legs.

"This is a change," Erek said. "I'm usually the one giving you guys some bad news."

"You want bad news?" Rachel said. "Ax is no better, and we can't figure out how to get into the Yeerk pool."

"Do you know anything about Andalite physiology?" I asked Erek.

He shrugged. Or at least caused his holographic self to shrug. "Nothing."

"Are any of your people surgeons?" I asked.

Erek shook his head. "The guy who plays my father? He was a doctor back in fifteenth-century France. He knows nothing useful, trust me."

"Erek, does the Yeerk pool have toilets?" Marco demanded suddenly.

"Marco, not the time," Jake muttered.

"Marco," Rachel warned, "be useful, or shut up."

"Come on. It's practically like a city down there," Marco continued. "They must have a place for the human hosts to take a leak or get a drink of water," he insisted.

"Sinks, toilets. They've got the works, sure," Erek answered.

The Chee are heavily programmed against violence. But that doesn't mean they don't hate the Yeerks. And they are the best spies you can imagine.

"That means they have plumbing. Pipes. And that also means we have a way into the Yeerk pool," Marco announced. "We morph into something small, something that can swim. Climb in one of our toilets, have Erek give us a flush, swim a little, and come out in one of the Yeerk sinks or toilets."

"Oh, yeah, that should work," Rachel said. "What are you, nuts?"

<The water pressure would be pretty hard to swim against,> Tobias commented.

Jake lifted his head. "Not if we started from the water tower. Then we'd go *with* the pressure all the way." He started to sound a little excited. His eyes glittered. "Erek, can you tap into the city water department computers? Combine it

40

with . . ." Jake sighed and wiped his mouth. "Combine it, with, um, with all you know about the Yeerk pool and . . . you know . . ."

"And give you a map? Directions?" Erek nodded. "I can give you directions to any sink or toilet in the place." He pointed at the computer my father and I use to keep records on the animals. "Mind?"

"There's no modem," I said.

Erek smiled. "Not necessary. I can be a modem."

Marco shot a triumphant glance at Rachel. "See? Still think my idea is nuts?" His face darkened. "Wait a minute. It *is* nuts. What's the matter with me? Am I insane?"

<Do we have a morph that could work?> Tobias asked.

"Maybe cockroach," I answered.

Jake shook his head. "There's a lot of pipe between the water tower and the Yeerk pool. I know they don't need to breathe much, but they do need to breathe eventually."

Tobias said, <I have an idea. Eels. They have them in tubs behind the bait shop. They're thin. And they're pretty fast, I think. Tasty.>

When I made a face, he said, <Hey, you think it's easy catching a mouse every day?>

"Eels? Do it," Jake ordered. A second later, Tobias was gone.

"Come on, Erek. We'll show you Ax's stall where we want you to do the hologram," Marco said.

Ax was asleep. He shuffled his feet in the hay as we crowded around the low stall door, but he didn't wake up. I did a quick temperature check on him.

Ninety-five point seven. Not much of a drop. Good. He wasn't close to the crisis point yet.

"I think the best thing is for me to stay in the stall with Ax," Erek said. "I can project a hologram around us both."

He slipped into the stall and closed the door behind him. A moment later, it was like he and Ax had disappeared. The stall looked completely empty.

I leaned my head over the stall door. The air shimmered around me, then Erek and Ax appeared.

"Thanks for doing this, Erek," I said.

"No prob," he answered.

"Don't you want a book to read in there?" I asked. "It's going to be boring."

"I have several thousand books stored in my brain. Sometimes I pass the time by seeing how many I can read and comprehend at the same time."

"Ooookay. Forget I asked."

I pulled my head out of the stall. I took a closer look at the hologram protecting Ax and Erek. No wrinkle or ripple or shadow to make my dad suspicious.

Unless he tried to go inside.

He won't, I told myself. He'd be too busy taking care of all the sick animals in cages to go poking around in an empty stall. I hoped.

"I just had a thought," Marco said.

"I'll buy you a card to commemorate the moment." Rachel, of course.

Marco didn't bother with a comeback. "If Ax goes into delirious mode, he could go running into town with underpants on his head or something. Erek won't be able to stop him."

He was right. The Chee aren't programmed for violence. Any kind of violence.

I looked at Jake. When stuff like this comes up, we all pretty much look at Jake.

Jake dropped his head back and closed his eyes for a long moment. Then he made his decision. "We've got to risk it. If something goes wrong at the Yeerk pool, it might take all of us to fight our way out."

I heard the flap of wings. Something oily slithered down my shoulder, then plopped onto the barn floor.

<Sorry,> Tobias apologized. <I dropped that

43

thing eight times on the way back. Lost the other one completely.>

"Hence slippery as an eel," Marco joked. "By the way, what with this being a crisis and all, I'm not even going to mention the sheer, bizarre, utter stupidity of taking a long ride through the city water supply. . . . But, just for the record, this is insane!"

He picked up the eel and held it for a moment, absorbing its DNA. Then he handed it to Rachel. When she was finished, she handed it to Jake. He held it briefly, focusing, then passed it to me.

"Did you get it already?" I asked Tobias.

<Yeah,> he said. <Eels. Why don't I just keep my mouth shut? Slimy little thing. Looks like a Yeerk.>

I glanced around the group. "I feel like we're missing someone," I said.

Then it hit me. Really hit me.

Ax. We'd be doing this mission without Ax.

CHAPTER 8

An hour later Jake, Rachel, Marco, and I were treading water inside the water tower that sits in a corner of the mall parking lot, shivering in the cold water.

You've seen the water towers I'm talking about: usually painted sky-blue. Steel. Four long legs and a big steel tank on top.

It was not high-tech. Basically they pump water up into the tower, and gravity lets it run down to homes and businesses and the girls' bathrooms at schools.

It was dark in the tank. Like being in a big swimming pool on the darkest night. Creepy. Except that this was the easy part.

I kept repeating Erek's instructions. The precise number of large pipes, water mains, we'd pass by on left and right. The elbow turns. The main we had to turn into. Then the downward elbow, the smaller turnoffs, and finally the long vertical drop that would signal we were descending to the Yeerk pool.

It was too much detail. Ax would have remembered it all. But Ax wasn't with us.

"Okay, remember, the pipes are just a road. Lots of turns and twists, but if we follow Erek's instructions we'll come out in a pipe that feeds directly into the Yeerk pool. The tap is almost always open. The Yeerk pool sludge is largely composed of water." Jake was trying to keep everyone calm. But he didn't sound too calm himself.

"Somehow I'm gonna end up getting flushed," Marco said grimly. "There is going to be flushing involved."

"Let's just do this!" Rachel yelled impatiently. She sounded cold. I could barely see her in the faint light from the access door we'd left open.

I turned my attention to the eel DNA inside me. The sound of my teeth chattering distracted me a little.

Then the sound changed. It became higher and lighter. That's because my teeth were changing, multiplying, growing longer and thinner and razor sharp.

Morphing is totally unpredictable. It's not like your body starts changing with the top of your head and goes on down to your toes. Or that your whole body changes all together, like a movie in slow motion.

It's grosser than that. Weirder. Stuff pops out. Like the long, narrow fin that had appeared all the way down Jake's back.

Other stuff disappears. Like Rachel's blond hair, which just got sucked into her head like a whole bunch of spaghetti into a very hungry mouth.

Popping and shrinking is only part of the deal. My eyes shrank and rolled down to the tip of my nose. My nose and chin stretched out, out, out around my new needle teeth. My forehead collapsed.

My bones liquefied, and my body caved in on itself until it was pencil-thin. Arms collapsing into my sides. Legs withering away completely.

I felt a tickly, itchy feeling as a long fin sprouted all the way down my back and gills opened up behind my mouth.

Teeny-tiny scales popped up all over my new body like goose pimples. Then an oily, slippery goop drenched me, oozing from my own body.

47

<Everybody done? Then let's book. Straight out the hole in the bottom,> Jake ordered.

I caught a flash of movement to my right. Food. Live food!

Zip! Chomp!

<Hey! That would be my tail! Whoever just bit me, get a grip,> Tobias complained.

Man, for a scrawny little thing with a pencil body, eels are aggressive. The eel's instincts were telling me to bite anything that moved and ask questions later.

And eat. I wanted live food.

Then . . . Chomp! Sharp teeth bit into my midsection.

<Okay, everyone stop biting!> I yelled. <Including me!>

I clamped down on the eel brain, pushing the simple, screaming instincts away. No biting, I told myself. No biting.

But then, something moved and . . .

No! I stopped myself in the nick of time.

<I am one mad little worm,> Rachel said with a laugh. <This eel has serious attitude.>

<Let's just go,> Jake said.

I began to move with a fluid, shimmying motion. Muscles stretched on one side, tightened on the other. My body went left, right, left, right. My tail whipped back and forth.

Down and down. Maybe just thirty feet to a

human, but a long dive to an eel the length of someone's finger.

And, as we descended, I began to feel the current. We were at the bottom of a huge sink. We were going out through the drain. The water began to rotate, a tornado!

Around, around, faster and faster!

Then, suddenly . . .

WOOOOSH!

Straight down at a million miles an hour!

CHAPTER 9

Down!

Down through the hole, down a massive pipe, jet-black blankness all around. Nothing to see or smell or feel but the sensation of speed, of falling forever.

<Now *this* is a water slide,> Rachel said, laughing a bit hysterically.

I pulled some water into my mouth and pumped it over my gills. Had to remember to breathe.

I whipped my body back and forth as hard as I could. We were going fast. But I wanted to go faster. Otherwise I was just a projectile, unable to keep my head forward and tail back.

Suddenly, we were horizontal. But the speed didn't lessen. We were rocketing! Tearing along the pipe, blind, aware of nothing . . .

No, not quite nothing. There was sound. Rushing water boiling around every slight imperfection in the pipe. And ahead . . . ahead a different sound. Louder. Water —

<PIPE!> I yelled.

We had a millisecond to react. We were at the pipe. The current yanked at my body and pulled it to the right. I fought it with all the sinewy strength of the eel's body.

Then, we were past the water main.

<That was the first one,> Jake said. <Everyone stay sharp. A lot more coming up.>

We always heard them, but always almost too late. It was harrowing. A wrong turn and there would be no telling where we'd come out.

We had two hours in morph. If we ended up in some dead end, without an open faucet we'd be trapped inside the pipe. Trapped. Unable to demorph. Unable to get out.

We would spend the rest of our lives as eels.

<Don't think about it,> I told myself. But I guess I said it in thought-speak because Tobias asked, <Don't think about what?>

<Don't think about the fact that we could all end up trapped in a water supply tube heading to

some toilet in some abandoned building that no one ever flushes,> Marco said. <Shhh! Don't think about it!>

<Turn coming up,> Jake said. <Right turn. Then pass a left and take another right almost immediately. Then pass two and go left. We'll be there in a few seconds and the whole sequence will only take about three seconds. Don't think, don't talk, just react.>

Jake was in the lead. I was right behind him. Tobias right behind me, then Marco and Rachel.

Suddenly . . .

Turn! Pass! Right! Pass! Pass!

<Aaahhh!> Jake yelled.

I ran into him, his tail was flailing madly. He'd been sucked into the wrong pipe.

He was flailing, trying to back out, no time to turn . . .

Chomp!

I made a blind lunge. My razor teeth closed on tail.

<Hang on!> I yelled.

I felt Tobias pressing against me from behind.

<Tobias! Grab me!>

Sharp pain as Tobias clamped down on my tail. But now I couldn't swim. Tobias had me, but Tobias couldn't hold us against the current.

<Get Cassie!> Marco snapped, having quickly grasped what had to be done.

Chomp! Chomp!

Don't ask me how they even found me, but they did. I was bleeding and vaguely in pain. But now it was three eels holding on to me.

I contracted my body in a sudden, one-sided jerk. Jake was yanked back out of the pipe and into the main current.

<Thanks,> Jake managed to say.

<Okay, which way now?> Tobias asked.

<Um . . . I . . .> Jake hesitated. He sounded woozy. Really out of it. Had he been that scared?

Maybe so, but Jake had never failed to cope.

I got a flash of him sitting in the barn with his head in his hands. Then another flash of the way his eyes looked when Marco came up with his plan to get into the Yeerk pool. I'd thought his eyes glittered with excitement.

I would have slapped myself if I'd had hands.

Jake was sick.

CHAPTER 10

<I think Jake is sick. That's why he's so out of it. He's feverish.> I sent my thought-speak to Rachel, Tobias, and Marco. <And I'm afraid it may be what Ax has. If he starts having demorphing spasms —>

<He could get too big. He could get crushed in the pipes,> Rachel finished for me.

<That does it. We've got to get him out of here,> Marco said. <But how?>

<No. We're not aborting the mission,> Rachel shot back. <Marco and Cassie, you can deal with Jake. Tobias and I will go on.>

<What, you're the boss now?> Marco demanded.

<I can't remember if Erek said to take the third right after the second left or what,> Jake mumbled.

<It's okay, Jake. It's okay,> I reassured him.

<Yeah, I'm in charge,> Rachel asserted. <Someone has to be.>

<Yeah, I'm going to happily follow some deranged violence junkie.>

<You don't want me to be leader? Fine. How about Cassie? Or Tobias?>

<Stop. Please just stop!> I exclaimed. <You're acting like Jake's dead or something. He's right here.>

I opened up the thought-speak to include Jake. <Jake, I think you have the *yamphut*. What do you want us to do?>

There was a long moment of silence. <Jake? Did you hear me?> I finally asked.

<Let's get out of here.>

<Shouldn't two of us go on?> Rachel argued.

<I . . . I don't . . . No. No. We all get out,> Jake ordered.

<How? We're lost!> Marco said.

<I . . . I don't . . .> Jake said woozily.

I felt a wave of sick dread. We were lost. Lost in pipes that stretched for miles. Jake out of commission. No one with an idea.

<It's like air!> Tobias said suddenly.

<What?>

<Air currents,> he said. <Sometimes I fly at night. Back up in the canyons. You can't see the walls of the canyon, you can't see the opening of the canyon and it's hard to get enough altitude to —>

<The point?!> Marco snapped. <Is there a point?>

<The wind. It doesn't blow through canyon walls; it can only blow out through the opening. If you ride it, sooner or later, it'll take you out. Water is the same. Has to come out somewhere, right?>

<So what? We ride the current?> I asked.

<Yeah, yeah. We ride the current, going with the flow, wherever it's strongest. Simple.>

<Simple, this?> Marco muttered.

We rode. We had no concept of time. No idea where we were, how much time we had left in morph. We simply rode the current through blackness, swimming enough to keep control of our bodies.

Forever. It seemed like forever. Down. Up. Right. Left. With Jake quieter and quieter. Moving more slowly.

Then . . .

<Hear that?> Marco asked.

<Current is still strong,> Rachel said.

<Really loud, isn't —> I started to say, then a sudden vertical jerk and woooosh, down a curv-

56

ing, rough-walled pipe, a sudden crush of pressure and . . .

<Aaaaaahhhhhhhhh!>

No pipe! I was hurtling through the air!

My eel eyes weren't good for much, but they could see the fire.

The fire that was everywhere!

<Aaaahhhh!> The others exploded from the end of the nozzle.

We were five eels. Blown from the end of a fire hose, arcing through the air toward a burning building.

CHAPTER 11

Through the air!

Through a window.

Splat!

I hit, then skidded across a floor.

<Demorph!> Rachel yelled.

I didn't need any encouragement. The rush of water shoved me up against a stove. I was demorphing, water hammering me.

But I didn't mind the water. The alternative was fire.

My human eyes returned and instantly began to sting. I squinted, shielding my face with a slimy, vestigial hand. The others rose like horrible monsters from the swirling water.

We were in a kitchen. The main fire was in the living room. I saw stairs.

"Stairs," Jake gasped. "Up."

We staggered, a half-morphed bunch of nightmares, up the stairs, away from the fire. Other hoses must have been hammering through the upper windows because water came down the stairs like a waterfall.

We made it to the second floor. Jake leaned over the railing and threw up.

"I don't see anyone up here," Rachel gasped, choking on the smoke.

I nodded agreement. "Let's . . ." Then I started coughing. It didn't matter. We knew what to do.

I don't think anyone noticed the birds of prey tearing out of a back window, singed and wet.

We flew only a short way. Jake was too weak to stay in the air.

We landed and demorphed.

"Well, that was fun," Marco said. "Let's do that again, real soon."

"Must be this stupid *yamphut*," Rachel said, helping me to hold Jake up. "Jake was sick in eel form. Sick in human form, too."

<Yeah. And Ax got sick in his human morph,> Tobias added. He was overhead, making sure we weren't being watched or followed.

59

"We'll try again after school tomorrow," Jake told us when he stepped off the ladder. "If I'm not better, you'll have to go without me. I'm going home. Try to rest up."

"Marco and I will walk you," I volunteered.

"I'll morph to owl and fly back to the barn," Rachel told us. "Check on Ax. And I'll ask him what he knows about how the *yamphut* affects humans, then call you at Jake's."

Jake wiped his mouth with his sleeve. "You go back to the barn, too, Tobias. And stay there," he instructed. "Erek's hologram is good. But it's not enough. If Ax fights his way out of the stall, morph into something big and stop him. If his temperature gets close to —"

"Ninety-one point three," I told him.

"Right. Okay. Wow. Man, my mind is gone. This sucks. Like the flu. That's how it feels. Like I have to . . ."

He bent over and heaved.

"Like you have to chuck?" Marco suggested.

Marco and I each wrapped an arm around Jake's waist and headed off. Fortunately the water tower was on the same side of town as Jake's house. But it was still a long way.

Rachel and Tobias took off.

"You ever notice how many different ways there are to say 'throwing up'?" Marco asked as we passed Dunkin' Donuts, the first in the row of fast food places dotting the main street running through town. "There's vomiting, of course. Hurling. Tossing your cookies. Puking, a classic. Ralphing."

I was glad Marco was filling up the silence. Even though I thought he could have come up with a better topic.

"There's cascading. But I prefer the terms that are more real. Like blowing chunks. Spewing your guts."

Marco took a deep breath and kept on talking as we made our way past Taco Bell. "Tangoing with the toilet. That's a good one," he said reflectively. "Technicolor yawn."

Jake broke away from us, staggered over to the curb, and — fill in your favorite term for puking here.

"I give that a four," Marco told Jake. "Sorry, guy. But your projectile force was not where it should be."

Jake started to straighten up. Then his knees buckled. Marco and I reached him just before he hit the pavement.

Marco wrapped one of Jake's arms around his shoulders. I slid his other arm around me. Then Marco and I made a seat for Jake by linking hands underneath him.

Soon Marco and I were huffing and puffing too much to talk. We turned off the main street, heading deeper into the residential section. A few porch lights were on but it was pretty dark. And quiet, except for said huffing and puffing.

"Almost there," Marco panted.

We turned onto Jake's block. When we reached Jake's porch, we gently lowered him to his feet. He wobbled a little, but managed to stay upright.

"Don't let Tom see me. In case I morph," Jake muttered.

I raised my hand to knock, but Jake's mom opened the door before we even had time to knock.

"Jake has the flu," I lied.

"I know. I'm on the phone with Rachel." Jake's mom held up the cordless. "She said you were on the way."

"I think Jake's about to blow again," Marco exclaimed. He hustled Jake off down the hall toward the bathroom.

"Can I talk to Rachel for a sec?" I asked.

Jake's mom handed me the phone.

"Rachel? It's me," I said.

"Jake's lucky," Rachel told me. "Our *other* friend has a much, much *worse* case of the flu. Our other friend says he thinks Jake will just get the usual flu. You know, fever, throwing up, headache. Our friend has some long, partially delirious explanation that you don't want to hear."

"Great. That's a relief at least," I said wearily.

"The bad news is that we're probably all going to get sick, too. This strain of the flu is extremely contagious," Rachel continued. "Got to go. I think I just heard your parents' car."

I stood there. Staring at the phone in my hand.

If we all got sick, who was going to save Aftran? And who was going to operate on Ax?

CHAPTER 12

I scrubbed my hands with hot, soapy water. Then I used my elbow to open the operating room door.

"He's at the crisis point," Noah Wyle told me as I approached the patient. He slapped a shiny scalpel into my hand.

"You're going to be just fine," I told the patient.

"I trust you, Cassie," the patient answered.

It was my dad lying on the table under the green sheet.

"S-shouldn't he be anesthetized?" I stammered.

Noah Wyle looked shocked. "Not for a *yamphut* operation."

I took a deep breath, the disinfectant burning the inside of my nose. I placed the blade on my dad's forehead.

Tap, tap, tap.

I looked up and saw Jake, Marco, Rachel, and Tobias behind the glass of the observation room. They tapped on the glass and waved to me.

I turned my attention back to my dad. But it wasn't Dad on the table anymore. It was Ax. I didn't know where to make the incision. Was the *Tria* gland in the front of the head? The back?

Tap, Tap, Tap.

Why were they tapping again? Didn't they know this was a delicate operation? I needed to concentrate.

Tap, Tap, Tap.

The sound finally jerked me awake.

"Cassie, you're going to be late for school," my mom called. She gave another tap, tap on my door.

"I'm up!" I cried.

I stood and opened the middle drawer of my dresser. I pulled on the first pair of pants and top my fingers touched. Then I pulled on my socks and shoes, yelled good-bye to my parents, and grabbed a Pop-Tart on my way out.

I couldn't stop yawning. I felt as if I'd only gotten about fifteen minutes of sleep. Marco and I had taken turns watching Jake last night. Marco was there now. He would be until Tom left for school. We thought in his fever Jake might start talking about something that would prove fatal if Tom overheard.

So I'd spent half the night as a fly on Jake's wall. Buzzing outside to the bushes to do quick demorphs and remorphs.

Jake didn't say anything at all suspicious. Sick as he was, I think there was some part of him that knew how dangerous the wrong words could be.

I rushed straight to the barn and over to Ax's stall. I stuck my head inside. Ax blinked up at me with his lovely almond-shaped eyes. <Sorry,> he mumbled.

"I think he feels bad that he's sick when you need him," Erek explained.

He handed me a chart with a notation of Ax's temperature every hour. It had dropped during the night. But less than a degree. It was at ninety-four point four. We had to operate when it got to ninety-one point three. There was still some time.

I handed the chart back to Erek, and ran my hand down the soft fur on Ax's neck. "Even warriors get sick sometimes," I told him. "It's not your fault."

<I've told him that about a million times,> Tobias said from his usual spot in the rafters.

"I'll be late if I don't leave right now," I told them. "Tobias, you know where I am if you need me."

I turned and bolted outside.

I got to school about four minutes before the first bell. I headed straight to Rachel's locker.

I waited for her to show until it was about one minute to the bell. Then I decided to check my locker. Maybe Rachel had been waiting over there for me.

I trotted over. No Rachel.

I hurried back to her locker. No Rachel.

The first bell rang. I stood by Rachel's locker as the hallway started to thin out. When I was the last one there, I decided I had to head to class.

I slipped into my desk about one second before the second bell. I pulled out a notebook and a pencil, and tried to focus on what the teacher was saying.

But my mind was too full to take in any new information. I kept wondering how low Ax's temperature was now. And how Jake was doing. And where Rachel was.

At least I could answer that last question for myself. I raised my hand and asked permission to go to the bathroom.

My teacher wasn't too happy that I hadn't gone before class started, but she handed over the pass anyway.

I rushed out the door, past the bathroom, and down to Rachel's first class. I peered in the little square window.

Rachel was not inside.

I turned and headed to the pay phone outside the gym. When I got to the phone I punched in Rachel's number. Rachel's mom answered on the second ring.

"It's Cassie. Is Rachel there?" I blurted.

"Rachel just fell asleep," Rachel's mom told me. "She was throwing up half the night."

CHAPTER 13

When it was finally time for lunch, I rushed straight to the cafeteria. I scanned the tables for Marco.

I felt a tap on my shoulder and figured Marco had found me. I turned around and saw Mr. Tidwell standing there.

"We need to talk about the Spanish Club party," he said.

He was trying to sound calm. But I could hear the tension in his voice. That was okay, he was probably hearing tension in mine.

He led the way into an empty classroom and shut the door behind us. "Visser Three will be returning earlier than expected. Aftran's interrogation may begin as early as eight tonight. You have to act quickly."

As he spoke, I couldn't stop myself from staring at his mouth. A Yeerk was moving his lips. Controlling his tongue.

Was the Yeerk tightening the muscles in Mr. Tidwell's throat to create that sound of tension I'd picked up on? Was it all part of some plan to make me trust him? To make sure I convinced my friends to walk right into an ambush?

"Why did you come to me?" I asked suddenly. "You say you know all about us. So you must know Jake is our leader. Why not go to him?"

Mr. Tidwell sat down on the teacher's desk. "Aftran trusts you. Only you. She said you had proven yourself to her," Mr. Tidwell explained.

Illim, I mean. It was so hard to think of him as anything but Mr. Tidwell.

I wished Illim hadn't singled me out of the group. We should all be here. At least all of us who could be.

The only thing I could do was try and make sure I asked everything the others would ask if they were here. It wasn't hard to figure out what Marco would want to know.

"I have another question. What about Mr. Tidwell? The real, human Tidwell?"

"When I first entered Mr. Tidwell, I was not part of the peace movement," Illim admitted.

"He was an involuntary host. No. That is too nice a way to say it. He was my host, my slave."

His eyes looked a little more watery than usual. Could the Yeerks control functions that were involuntary for humans? Could the Yeerk just push a neuron or something and stimulate a host's tear ducts?

"It was partly experiencing Mr. Tidwell's distress that led me to join the movement," Illim continued. "His howls of fury and agony forced me to accept what I had done to him. At the same time I began to hear about a group of Yeerks who thought it was wrong to take an unwilling host."

I nodded. It made sense to me. Hearing the endless cries of another sentient creature, knowing you had caused its pain. How could that fail to have an effect?

Then I remembered something Aftran had told me. To most Yeerks, humans are like pigs. Just meat. Oink, oink.

"It didn't happen all at once," Illim continued. "But gradually I realized that I did not want to inhabit Mr. Tidwell's body if it meant sacrificing his freedom for mine.

"And now . . . now, Mr. Tidwell has something to say. I am repeating his thoughts as I hear them," Illim said.

"Can't you let him talk for himself?" I asked.

71

"I am speaking for myself," Tidwell said.

"How can I know that?"

"You can't."

I hesitated. "Okay. What do you want to say?"

"Cassie, I invited Illim to stay in my body," Mr. Tidwell explained. "I thought together we could do more for peace than he could do alone. He is within me now with my permission."

There was no change in his voice or manner. But there wouldn't be.

Tidwell swallowed hard. "My wife died a few years ago. For a long time, I didn't care about anything. I stumbled through my life. Getting myself to school. Getting home again."

He leaned forward, his eyes locked on my face. "When Illim gave me my freedom back, I realized I wanted to do something with it. So I decided to join the fight. What could be more important?" he said. "And Illim and I, we've become friends. He's actually very good company."

I didn't know if Marco and the others would believe that what I'd just heard was actually Mr. Tidwell and not some Yeerk trick. I wasn't sure I did.

But I wanted to believe it.

"Look, I want to help you," I told Mr. Tidwell/Illim. "But three members of the group are sick. Really sick. As in one requiring brain surgery. Isn't there some way the Yeerk peace movement can rescue Aftran without our help?"

"Illim speaking now," he told me. "The peace movement is growing. We now have nearly a hundred members. But not all the Yeerks in the movement have hosts. And not all the hosts the others have are suitable for battle."

Illim gave Mr. Tidwell's paunch a pat. "Can you imagine trying to fight Hork-Bajir in this?" he asked. "I'm sorry to hear that members of your group are ill. But when the Visser finishes with Aftran, he will know everything. And then every Yeerk in the peace movement will be dead. Their hosts as well. Everyone who has ever helped you will be rounded up and made Controllers," Illim continued. "Everyone you care about will be made Controllers. It will all end, Cassie. The defeat will be total, and permanent."

I sat down and just buried my face in my hands for a minute. I felt like my head was going to explode. This was hopeless! An impossible rescue with half our strength gone?

But there was no alternative.

"Okay," I said at last. "If we can do it, we'll do it."

I pushed myself to my feet and started to the door on shaky legs. Then . . . then an idea . . .

I paused, and turned back.

"Illim, if you had to survive for a few hours outside Mr. Tidwell, could you? Without being in the Yeerk pool, I mean," I asked.

"As long as I stayed in some kind of liquid environment," he answered. He sounded a little puzzled.

But I wasn't puzzled. Not anymore. I had a plan.

A totally terrifying plan.

But a plan.

CHAPTER 14

"Hey, Marco. Wait up." I chased down the street until I caught up to him. I'd been hoping I'd find him on his way home from school. "I talked to Tidwell. Visser Three is coming back early."

"Do you remember 'Five Little Monkeys'?" Marco asked me, grinning a loopy grin.

"Did you hear me?" I demanded. "We've got to get Aftran out *today*. But I think I have a plan."

"It was a song. More of a chant, I guess. With little hand gestures," Marco continued. Totally ignoring me.

"It went like this." Marco began talking in a rhythmic singsong. "'Five little monkeys jumping on the bed. One fell off and broke his head. Mama called the doctor and the doctor said —' "

I chanted the last line with Marco. " 'No more monkeys jumping on the bed.' Yeah, yeah, can we move on?"

"Then it would start again. Except with four little monkeys jumping on the bed," Marco said.

I circled around in front of him and walked backward so I could look at him while I talked. "I remember it. Now, do you want to play jump rope or do you want to hear my plan?"

"We're the five little monkeys," Marco said, staring me in the eye. "Well, six. Three of us already fell off the bed. Now there are only three of us left. Monkey Cassie. Monkey Tobias. And Monkey Marco."

He gave a few halfhearted oooh-oooh-ooohs and scratched himself under the arms cartoon monkey-style.

"You're scared, aren't you?" I asked. I dropped back into step beside him.

"Yeah, I'm scared. Of course I'm scared," he shot back. "Ax could die. And we're getting ready to go into the Yeerk pool with half our usual fighting force. Half! That is unless another one of us keels over in the next couple hours. Which could happen."

"You're feeling okay so far though, right?" I

asked. I reached out and pressed my wrist against his forehead.

Kind of warm. Kind of clammy.

But we'd been walking. Marco had probably just worked up a sweat.

"My eyes feel kind of weird. Kind of gummy," Marco admitted. "But they showed a film in Health today."

"That could do it."

"I guess now that Rachel's out of it, I get to be in charge," Marco said.

"Yep. You're the man," I answered.

"So since I'm the leader, I should hear about this plan of yours then," he said. Marco shifted his backpack to the opposite shoulder. Then switched it right back.

"I talked to Mr. Tidwell at lunch. He told me himself he's willingly participating in the Yeerk peace movement. He thinks it's the most important work he could do," I explained. Marco didn't jump in with any nasty comment, so I kept talking. "Illim, Mr. Tidwell's Yeerk, told me he could survive for several hours if he's in liquid. He doesn't have to be in the Yeerk pool or anything."

I took a deep breath. "I thought I could morph him, and —"

"You want to morph a *Yeerk*?" Marco demanded. He started to make loud barfing noises.

"I know it's kind of desperate, but . . ."

My voice trailed off as Marco leaned into the bushes and threw up.

I moved up behind him and rested my hand on his back. Finally Marco's back stopped heaving. He straightened up and wiped his mouth with his sleeve. Then he turned to face me.

"Another monkey just fell off the bed," he said. Then, with a crooked smile, he added, "Poor Cassie."

I tried to smile bravely. But I wasn't feeling brave. I was feeling scared and alone.

"Got to think about one thing," Marco said weakly.

"What?"

"What if . . . what if you pull it off?"

Then he collapsed. And I was too busy hauling him back up to his feet to think about what he'd just said.

Only later did it occur to me. Marco had seen the fatal flaw.

If I succeeded. If I rescued Aftran. Then what? I'd have an outlaw Yeerk, without a host, and worse by far, without access to life-giving Kandrona rays.

I could save Aftran. Only to watch her die.

CHAPTER 15

<Ax's temperature is down to ninety-two point eight,> Tobias announced from his perch as I rushed into the barn.

I did a little math in my head. I'd been gone for about nine hours. Ax's temperature had gone down one point six degrees. So he was losing not quite two points an hour. So we had about eight hours before he hit the crisis.

"Visser Three's coming back tonight," I told Tobias. I filled him in on my conversation with Mr. Tidwell and my plan.

"I should make it back from the Yeerk pool before Ax needs us to operate," I said.

If I made it back.

I started toward Ax's stall.

<Problem,> Tobias said. <His temperature has been dropping all day. His crisis could happen tonight, or a few hours from now, or basically now. I haven't been able to figure out a pattern. Sometimes it drops slow, sometimes fast.>

"You might have to do it yourself. The surgery," I said. "You'll have to try to get Ax to tell you where the gland is. You can use that little room my dad uses when he has to set bones and stuff. There are supplies in there."

<So, Rachel and Marco?> Tobias asked.

"Yeah," I answered.

<If I have to do it myself, I have to do it myself,> Tobias said. <Try to finish saving the world early. You know more about medicine and stuff than I do.>

"I'll skip the post-saving-the-world party," I promised.

I wanted to be here when Ax hit the crisis. But I wasn't sure I'd be able to do much more than Tobias could. Yeah, I knew how to splint a bird's broken wing and stuff a pill down a raccoon's throat.

But that wasn't brain surgery. Not even close.

One cut in the wrong place, and Ax could lose his ability to thought-speak. Or breathe. It would be so easy to cause him permanent damage. So easy to kill him.

How could I live knowing I had killed a friend?

That reminded me of Aftran. She was a friend, too. And pulling her out of the Yeerk pool meant excruciating Kandrona starvation unless I could think of a solution.

I didn't know how Jake did it. How did he make life-or-death decisions and not go insane with guilt and grief?

<Maybe I'll go check on the other patients,> Tobias said, pulling me out of my thoughts.

"You should," I said. He wanted to check on Rachel. "I need to head out in about an hour."

<I'll be back before then,> he promised. He beat wings out the hayloft window.

I hurried over to Ax's stall. When I opened the door, Ax and Erek appeared in front of me.

"How are you guys doing?" I asked them.

<Erek has been teaching me how to play Rock, Scissor, Paper. Rock smashing scissor I understand,> Ax said. <And scissor cutting paper. But not paper wrapping rock. Rocks do not breathe, correct? So how would this hurt them?>

"Paper beating rock. It is sort of weird," I answered.

<Weird, yes. That is why I now owe Erek one million and seven dollars,> Ax told me.

I raised my eyebrows at Erek. He shrugged.

<One million and seven dollars. Is that a great deal of money?> Ax asked.

"It's up there," I answered, giving his arm a quick pat.

Ax pointed his stalk eyes toward the barn roof. <I don't see it up there,> he said.

"I mean it's a lot. A lot of money," I explained.

Ax kept his eyes focused upward. <Wait. Now I think I see it. I'll go get it.> He took a step forward and a spasm raced through his body.

"That's okay," Erek said. "Don't worry about it. We'll play more later, and you'll win the money back from me."

Ax didn't answer. He just kept staring at the ceiling.

Erek leaned close to me. "He's been like this all day," he whispered. "He'll seem okay. And then he loses it."

So he was still delirious part of the time.

"Any close calls with my dad?" I asked. I glanced at the stall door. From this side, the hologram looked like a smoky silver cloud. I could only see faint shapes and shadows out in the barn.

"Tobias had to buzz the cages once. The animals all freaked, and that kept your dad busy," Erek answered.

"Just tell me you're not going to get this stupid illness."

Erek smiled. "I've never been sick a day in my life. And I am really, really old."

I turned my attention to Ax. "Ax. Hey, Ax. Come on, stop staring up there. I need you to talk to me."

Ax slowly lowered his eye stalks.

"Can you tell me where the *Tria* gland is? Can you point to the spot on your head?" I asked.

<You said the test wouldn't cover the *Tria* gland,> Ax complained. <You said we didn't have to know the glands.>

Oh, man. He thought he was back in school.

"This isn't a test, Ax. You're not going to be graded or anything," I tried to reassure him. "Just take a guess. Where do you think the *Tria* gland is? I need to know."

Thump. Thump. Thump.

Erek grabbed my shoulder and pointed into the barn. A dark shadow moved closer.

It was my dad thumping through the barn in his clunky work boots. And he was heading right for us.

I threw myself at the stall door and scrambled over. It had to look like I had materialized out of thin air.

"You don't have to do a thing out here," I

blurted. "I already fed and watered all the animals myself."

My dad peered over my shoulder. "Where were you hiding? I was sure the barn was empty when I came in."

"I was right here the whole time. Got to get those bifocals, Dad," I said.

My dad frowned. "You can't fool me, Cassie," he told me. "I know you were in that empty stall. And why."

My heart gave a hard double thump.

"You do?" I asked.

He nodded. "You were pretending you were a horse, weren't you?" he asked.

I hadn't played that game where I pretended I was a horse since I was about five. Okay, maybe six.

But I didn't tell my dad that. I just gave him a weak smile. "Yeah. You caught me."

CHAPTER 16

As soon as I got my dad out of the barn, I fed and watered the animals. I had to since I'd said I'd already done it.

Then I headed to the corner of the barn where my dad has a little workbench. He's not Joe Carpenter, but he did go through a spell where he was really into making birdhouses. Plus he makes cages sometimes and does repairs around the barn. So he had a decent selection of tools.

I knew my dad had most of the stuff I would need for the *Tria* gland surgery in the operating room. But I didn't think he'd have anything I could use to cut through Ax's skull. My dad's a great vet, but he doesn't saw through bone much.

I scanned the messy array of tools. Was there anything that could cut through bone?

My dad had a saw with teeth I thought could handle the job. But the saw was way too long. Unless I was going to cut Ax's head straight down the middle like a big melon . . .

I squeezed my eyes shut against the gory image that popped into my mind. I tried to reassure myself. The *Tria* gland probably wasn't too big. I'd only need to make a small hole.

A small hole leading directly into Ax's brain. Somehow that thought wasn't all that comforting.

I ran my eyes over the tools again. There was a power drill. That would definitely be able to make a hole through bone. But the hole would be too small.

I saw a few more tools jammed behind a half-finished birdhouse. I picked it up, my fingers curling into the little round hole in the front.

Hmmm. That little hole was probably about the size of the one I needed to make in Ax's skull.

I remembered what tool my dad used to make it. It's called a hole saw. It looks sort of like a corkscrew. Except instead of a metal ring that fits around the top of a bottle, there is a little round saw.

I rushed to the operating room, clicked on the

fluorescent lights, and stashed the saw. Then I made a little pile of supplies I thought I might need: hemostats, retractors, scissors, syringes, surgical thread, cotton balls, bandages, betaine, alcohol.

As I headed out of the operating room I heard a flapping sound. Then Tobias swooped through the hayloft.

"How's Rach —" I began.

<Didn't get there,> he answered as he headed toward his usual perch in the rafters. <Started to feel . . .>

His words trailed off as he dropped lower for his landing. And lower.

Way too low.

"Tobias, watch out!" I screeched.

THUMP!

Tobias ran into the rafter headfirst.

He plummeted.

THUD!

He landed on the barn floor. And lay still.

"No! No, no, no!" I raced over to Tobias and dropped to my knees beside him.

Gently I scooped him up. I couldn't tell which was trembling. His body. Or my fingers holding his body.

"Tobias, are you okay?" I crooned.

He didn't answer.

"Tobias? Tobias!"

<I swear I didn't drink the punch,> he answered.

A little groggy. But definitely alive.

I slowly climbed to my feet, careful to keep from jarring him, and started toward the row of cages. "I'm going to have to put you next to a golden eagle. I know you hate them, but it's the only room available right now."

Tobias gave a weak flutter in my hands. <What are you doing?> he demanded.

"I'm going to get my dad to take care of you," I answered. I slid him into the empty cage and latched the door.

<You're locking me up? No way!> Tobias cried. <I want out of here!> He struggled to his feet and puffed his feathers.

I grabbed a chart and noted that the red-tailed hawk appeared disoriented. I added that I thought it had stunned itself flying into one of the rafters.

If there were other symptoms, my dad would know how to handle them. At least I didn't have to worry about Tobias.

I had to worry about Ax more. If he went into crisis while I was at the Yeerk pool, there would be no one to operate.

Tobias gnawed on one of the cage's metal bars with his beak. "Oh, just stop it," I snapped.

"You're in the best place you can possibly be. I have no time, no time, NO TIME for any crap, okay?!"

<Okay,> he said meekly.

"Yes, ma'am," Erek said from the last stall.

I tried to get a grip on myself. I took a couple of deep breaths. Didn't work. I wasn't calm.

CHAPTER 17

Tobias was right, I thought as I rushed into the house. I was the leader now. The leader of one. The last little monkey jumping on the bed.

I found my mom sitting at the computer. "I'm doing a report on animal brain surgery," I told her. "Any books you think might help?"

"Hmm." My mother reached out and pulled a thick green book off the shelf over her head. "The introductory chapter in this one is pretty good." She grabbed a thinner volume. "And this one has some good photos."

I took them from her. "Thanks. Rachel has the flu. I told her I'd keep her company a while, okay?"

"Well, don't you get it," she said. She grabbed her coffee cup and took a swallow.

I remembered the day she got that cup. She and my dad and I were at the amusement park part of The Gardens. They have one of those photo booths where you get your face put onto another body. We decided on all three of us as super models. My mom thought it was so hilarious she had it put on the cup.

She and I always teased my dad about how he was the prettiest of the three of us. He'd always laugh and give us these outrageous beauty tips.

"I'll tell her," I said. Lying, the way I've had to lie so often since that day Elfangor gave us the power to morph.

"Um, bye." I wished I could say something else, something more. It could be the last time I —

I rushed out of the house and back to the barn. I headed to Ax's stall. I took a deep breath, then stepped inside.

"How are you doing, Ax?" I asked.

One of his stalk eyes swung a half turn toward me. That was all the reaction I got.

"I just took his temperature again. Ninety-one point nine," Erek said.

It had dropped almost a whole degree in less than an hour. If it continued falling at this rate there was no possible way I'd be back in time.

Tobias said there was no pattern to the way the temperature fell. I had to hope that it would slow down now.

"Erek, Tobias is sick now, too. I had to put him in one of the cages," I told him. "If Ax reaches his crisis before I get back . . ."

I really didn't want to say this. But I had to.

"You can't go to my father or anyone else for help," I finished.

What I was really telling Erek was he had to let Ax die.

Erek nodded. "I understand."

If Ax was lucid, he'd understand, too. I knew he would. Ax was a trained warrior-cadet. He'd know that sometimes one member of a team had to be sacrificed to save the rest.

I turned to Ax and rested my palm against his forehead. "Can you hear me, Ax?" I asked.

I felt him move the tiniest bit under my hand. Had he heard me? Was he trying to answer? I couldn't be sure.

"Sorry, Ax," I whispered. "I'd stay with you if I could."

I felt hot tears sting my eyes and I blinked them away.

"You understand, don't you?" I continued. "I have to try and save all of us. Not just you."

I slowly slid my hand away from his forehead.

Then I turned and rushed out of the stall without another word.

I grabbed my bike from its spot propped beside the barn door. I hopped on and pedaled hard. I wasn't going far. Good, old-fashioned, normal bike would be easiest.

I pedaled away from Ax and Tobias and Erek. Away from my parents. Away from Jake, Marco, and Rachel.

I was all alone.

I slammed my feet down on the pedals. Trying to burn off some of the fear building inside me.

Trying to block out all the "what ifs."

What if I didn't get back before Ax reached his crisis?

What if my plan didn't work? What if I got sick before I could save Aftran?

What if I screwed up?

What if? What if? What if?

What if I had killed Aftran when I had the chance?

I slowed down as I thought about that one.

I'd been alone when I faced that moment, too. Alone, I had made the choice to let Aftran live.

It had turned out to be the right choice.

Aftran hadn't betrayed me or the other Animorphs. She'd gone on to do important work in the Yeerk peace movement.

If I got Aftran out of the Yeerk pool before the Visser interrogated her, the peace movement would continue. The Animorphs would continue to fight.

If I failed . . .

CHAPTER 18

I rode my bike up Mr. Tidwell's driveway and parked it. Then I hurried to his front door. He swung it open before I had the chance to ring the bell.

"Where are the others?" he demanded.

"Sick."

"It's just you?"

"Yes. Me. Me or no one."

He hesitated only a moment, then he drew me inside.

"So where should we do this?" he blurted the second I was inside. "Bathroom? Kitchen? Where?"

He kept touching his ear, rubbing his finger

around the edge. He seemed totally freaked by what we were about to do.

I felt like telling him to join the club. But I figured that would only make things worse.

"Kitchen's fine," I answered. I led the way, even though it was his house. Even though he was a teacher and I was a kid. There wasn't time to waste on all that.

I sat down at the kitchen table and waved Mr. Tidwell down into the chair next to me. "Now?" he asked.

"Let's do it!" I said.

It was Rachel's line. But Rachel wasn't there. Maybe it would bring us luck. All of us.

Mr. Tidwell tilted his right ear toward the table.

I leaned down. My eyes locked themselves on the hole at the ear's center. I couldn't look away.

The opening to the hole began to glisten. Then a pencil-thin wand of wet gray flesh slid out. It wiggled this way and that. Almost as if it were tasting the air.

Shh-lop. Shh-lop. Shh-lop.

More of the gray flesh squeezed itself out of Mr. Tidwell's ear.

Plop!

The Yeerk fell the few inches to the table. Its body had been stretched and flattened by crawling out the ear canal.

As I watched, the Yeerk's gray flesh contracted, like a hand closing into a fist. Forming its slug-like body.

I jerked back. The legs of my chair squealed against the kitchen floor.

It's Illim, I told myself, trying to control my revulsion.

Mr. Tidwell grabbed a dishtowel from the table and scrubbed at his ear. "It always makes me feel . . . I don't know. Empty."

I didn't answer. I wanted to move. I didn't want to have too much time to think about what I was about to do.

I reached out and gently rested my fingertips on Illim's squishy flesh. I closed my eyes. Focused. And the DNA of the Yeerk became a part of me.

The Yeerk. The Yeerk became part of me.

I pulled my fingers away from Illim. Mr. Tidwell filled a Ziploc bag with water and slipped Illim inside. Then he closed the top almost all the way and carefully placed the bag in the big patch pocket of his corduroy jacket.

"You know if something goes wrong, Visser Three could find out I'm the one who brought you in," he said. "If that happens, he'll kill us."

"Yeah, well, he's been trying to do that for a long time, but here I am," I said. Then I laughed at my own bravado.

Mr. Tidwell smiled. "You were always a good student. Unlike Jake, who never completely applies himself."

I sighed. "Well, I wish Jake were here now. It's time. I have to do this. It's kind of gross to watch."

"I think I can handle it."

I focused my mind. The changes began.

Any morph is frightening. Any new morph doubly so.

This morph . . . this was the enemy. This was a parasite. This was a slug.

My skin turned slick with a thin coat of mucus. It covered my entire body, oozing from the pores.

My eyelids.

The spaces between my fingers and my toes.

My neck, my legs, my stomach.

The mucus thickened into a goo like half-set Jell-O. It seeped into my ears. My nose. My mouth.

I gagged as the mucus swelled in my mouth. My teeth began to dissolve, as if the mucus was an acid.

My lips melted together, closing my mouth on vanishing teeth and swelling goo.

Ax always says I'm the best morpher. But it was hard not to resist this morph.

I tried to relax. To give myself over to the changes.

My body turned cold as the thick slime slid down my throat, packing my esophagus. Somehow I was still breathing. Maybe through my skin.

A wave of nausea rolled through me as the cold, thick mucus hit my stomach and intestines. I felt them shrivel up and disappear.

The mucus wrapped itself around my heart. And my heart withered and stopped beating.

Slime stuck my arms to my sides and glued my legs together. I felt it seep through my flesh until it hit bone. The cold slime turned my bones to ice. Then they shattered into a zillion pieces.

The floor rushed up to meet me as I fell off the chair. I hadn't begun to shrink yet, and I lay there, the world's largest slug. My entire body made up of slick, squishy flesh.

Only my eyes remained unchanged. They stared straight up at the ceiling.

Mr. Tidwell appeared above me. His face contorted in horror. I think he was screaming. I couldn't hear him.

His face became cloudy as mucus coated my eyes. His face disappeared as my eyes dissolved completely.

Then my body curled in on itself. Tightening, tightening. Becoming smaller and smaller.

Falling . . . Falling . . .

And it was over. The transformation complete.

I was a Yeerk.

CHAPTER 19

I lay on Mr. Tidwell's kitchen floor. Deaf, blind, capable of only the slowest movement.

How would I even be able to find Mr. Tidwell's ear? I had no idea, but the Yeerk would know. I tried to open myself up to the Yeerk instincts and let them guide me.

I realized that I could do something kind of like a bat's echolocation. Or like sonar. The Yeerk threw out some kind of electrical waves, then analyzed the way they were bounced back at it. That gave it an idea of the size and shape of things.

My sonar picked up an object, bigger than I was, moving in. I felt warmth surround me, and I was lifted up, up, up.

My sonar picked up a new shape. My Yeerk instincts kicked in. Hard. I stuck out two little protrusions. Felt around until I targeted the small opening.

Then I was moving in. Slithering right into Mr. Tidwell's ear canal. It was a tight fit. I squirted out some kind of painkiller to deaden the canal and squirmed, stretched, pushed bones and tissue aside with surprising strength.

I penetrated. Deeper. Puncturing flesh now. Deeper inside.

I inched along until I felt the faint tingle of electricity.

Yes! This was what I was looking for.

The brain!

The neurons fired microvolts around me as I stretched. I was paper-thin. Spread like hammered-down Silly Putty.

I pressed myself into the cracks and crevices of the brain.

Ah! Now I could feel it. The neurons were connecting to me. Making me a part of this strange, wondrous new body.

I felt the Yeerk's jolt of awe and pleasure at its new mobility. At its new size, and strength, and power. It was a visceral, nonconscious, nonintellectual, animal pleasure.

I touched the brain's center of hearing.

Ahhhh! It was like being alive again. The

sound of water dripping into the sink sounded beautiful.

Then, I touched the centers for sight.

It was lights-on after being forever in a mine shaft. Overwhelming! Joyful! It was dazzling, dizzying delirium.

Aftran was so right when she told me humans live amidst splendor and magnificence. Mr. Tidwell's red-and-white-checked tablecloth was a sight to be relished and lingered over. The —

<Cassie. Cassie, what are you doing? We have to leave!> I heard a voice call.

Mr. Tidwell. Speaking only in thought.

<Can't you figure out how to move my body?> he asked, sounding panicked.

I could have stood in Mr. Tidwell's kitchen all night. Allowing myself to feel the Yeerk's joy at every new sensation.

But I had a job to do. And not much time. I clamped down on my Yeerk desire to explore the new world.

I wasn't sure how to use the connections between me and Mr. Tidwell to control him. But the Yeerk knew.

I allowed it to open sections of Mr. Tidwell's brain. Some sections controlled physical functions like moving muscles. But some held memories.

As I tapped into these areas I was flooded with images from Mr. Tidwell's life.

Mr. Tidwell sitting in this kitchen, the sink overflowing with dirty dishes. The counters spattered with food stains. The smell of garbage heavy in the air.

A younger, thinner Mr. Tidwell in this same kitchen, but now sparkling clean and cheerful, standing next to his wife, flicking soapsuds at her.

Mr. Tidwell walking into a classroom on his first day as a teacher. Feeling proud and nervous as he wrote his name on the board and turned to face the class.

Mr. Tidwell climbing into his bed last night, and carefully placing his wife's picture on the pillow beside him.

I didn't want to see that. I didn't want to go pawing through Mr. Tidwell's memories. I wished I could apologize to him, but even though I could hear his thoughts, I didn't know how to send him my thoughts back.

I continued searching his brain, backing away any time I hit memory. But memory was everywhere. I was invading every secret, destroying all privacy.

I felt ashamed.

I tried to move a hand. It moved.

I tried to form speech. It was easy.

"Okay, I think I've got it," I muttered in Mr. Tidwell's voice.

I took a step — and bumped into the table.

<Don't worry. I'm kind of klutzy,> Mr. Tidwell said.

I appreciated him trying to joke.

I took another step. Didn't hit anything.

I slowly headed out the front door, feeling more at ease in my new body with every motion. I climbed into Mr. Tidwell's car. I didn't know how to drive, but Mr. Tidwell did. And anything he knew how to do, I now knew how to do.

I pulled the keys out of Mr. Tidwell's pocket, turned on the ignition, and pulled out onto the street.

It was pretty cool driving by myself. I was kind of sorry when we pulled into the McDonald's parking lot. For more reasons than one.

Usually I'd be listening to Jake give last-minute instructions right now. I'd be laughing at the jokes Marco tells right before we do something insanely dangerous.

Tobias would probably be flying overhead, giving his version of an aerial traffic report. Rachel would be getting all macho, her bravery bolstering mine.

I was hit again by how alone I was. I missed them. I missed them so much.

I climbed out of the car and made my way into McDonald's. I was aware of how the new smells and colors and sounds interested the

Yeerk part of me but I didn't allow myself to get distracted.

I got in the line closest to the bathrooms. When the girl behind the register asked for my order I told her I wanted a Happy Meal with extra happy.

The girl gave a fake laugh, like she'd heard the joke a billion times. Which I knew she had. Asking for extra happy was the password to the Yeerk pool.

I guess Yeerks have a sense of humor.

Mr. Tidwell had the drill down pat. That meant I did, too. I walked past the bathroom and opened the next door, which led into the kitchen. I went straight into the walk-in refrigerator.

WHOOSH! The back of the fridge split and slid open.

I knew the Gleet BioFilter was just inside. I took a deep breath and stepped through.

The BioFilter didn't make a single Brrrr-EEEET. All it detected was human and Yeerk. Both authorized life-forms.

It had no way of sensing the Animorph who was also making her way through the entrance to the Yeerk pool.

CHAPTER 20

I started down the long staircase leading to the Yeerk pool. The air felt moist against my face. Almost oily.

Mr. Tidwell's glasses clouded up. I pulled them off and everything went soft and blurry. I quickly wiped them on the hem of my shirt and stuck them back on. I couldn't see without them.

It was so strange to be in someone else's human body. To have it feel so different. Even the sound his body's footsteps made sounded strange. Too loud and heavy.

I descended the stairs down to the Yeerk pool.

I found myself wishing my steps made even more noise. I wanted to drown out the sounds drifting up from below me. The screams of fury.

The howls of agony. And underneath them all, the low sobs of pure despair.

I knew exactly who was making those horrifying, soul-slashing sounds. Around the edge of the Yeerk pool are cages filled with the involuntary hosts, human and Hork-Bajir.

They screamed, threatened, howled, and sobbed because they could. For a few hours their voices were their own again as their Yeerks swam in the pool, soaking in Kandrona rays and other nutrients. Soaking up life.

I forced myself to continue down the stairs. The earth walls around me changed to rock. And the purple glow at the bottom of the staircase grew stronger.

Down, down, down.

The cries of the hosts grew louder. And I began to hear the sound of the sludge swooshing against the shore of the pool.

The rock walls widened. I was almost there.

Down, down, down.

I took the last few steps, and entered the huge cavern. It was like a small city. Humans, Taxxons, Hork-Bajir everywhere. Buildings and sheds in a ring around the outside. Bright yellow Caterpillar earthmovers and tall cranes ready to continue the underground expansion.

Expansion. The idea made my stomach cramp.

<Go join the line at the closest pier,> Mr. Tidwell instructed. <The line at the second pier is for reinfestation.>

As I started toward the pier, I heard the most horrifying sound yet. The sound of laughter. I scanned the cavern, looking for the source.

A group of humans was watching a *Full House* rerun in a room along the back wall.

They were the voluntary hosts. The ones who had chosen to allow Yeerks to control them. They were just hanging out watching TV while their Yeerks swam in the pool. Somehow they managed to tune out the screams and cries from the cages.

I turned away from them and continued to the pier. I took my place in line. There were three humans and one Hork-Bajir ahead of me.

How long would this take? I had to get Aftran out before the Visser returned.

The first human, a boy who looked about five, stepped to the end of the pier. He calmly knelt down and the two Hork-Bajir-Controllers helped him lower his head into the iron-gray sludge of the Yeerk pool.

I knew the moment the Yeerk slid out of the boy's ear. His feet started to kick against the metal pier. Wham! Wham! Wham!

The Hork-Bajir-Controllers yanked him up.

The boy opened his mouth wide. "Mommeeee!" he screamed.

The horrible high-pitched call made the hair on the back of my — Mr. Tidwell's — neck stand on end. The hair on my arms, too.

Two more Hork-Bajir-Controllers marched down to the end of the pier. They took the boy away from the first two, and escorted him back toward the cages.

When they passed me, I wanted to reach out and snatch the little boy away from them. He should be whooshing down the slide at the playground. He should be learning the names of all the Crayola crayons in the big box.

"Mommeeee!" the boy screeched again. "Mommeeee!"

I struggled to keep Mr. Tidwell's face expressionless as I heard a cage door clang shut behind me, locking the boy inside. If a flicker of concern crossed my face, we risked getting caught.

Illim must go through this all the time, I realized. He had to make sure he acted like a regular Yeerk. And that meant acting like his host's feeling meant nothing to him.

The next human in line, a tall, neatly dressed woman, knelt at the edge of the pier and lowered her head into the pool. She gave only the smallest twitch to indicate that the Yeerk had slithered out of her ear.

Then she stood up, straight and tall. Her eyes burned with hatred as the Hork-Bajir-Controllers marched her back to the cages. But she didn't make a sound.

The Hork-Bajir was next in line. As I watched it lower its head into the water, I couldn't help thinking of the tiny colony of free Hork-Bajir living in their secret valley.

The Hork-Bajir gave an anguished bellow as it raised its head. The gray sludge dripped into its open mouth.

I'm getting Aftran out of here, I promised myself. There was only one person left ahead of me in line. A short dark-haired man. He knelt. Submerged his head.

Then like the woman, he stood up without crying out or struggling. The two Hork-Bajir-Controllers took him by the arms. The man walked two steps, then fell to his knees.

He must have surprised the Hork-Bajir-Controllers, because he managed to break free of them. He shoved himself to his feet and ran past me down the pier.

Go, go, go! I thought. But I was careful not to let the words escape my lips.

One of the Hork-Bajir-Controllers pulled out a Dracon beam. TSEEEWWWW! TSEEEWWWW!

I shot a glance over my shoulder in time to see the man fall to the ground, his singed clothes

111

smoking. He let out a low groan of pain, and I realized his skin had been singed, too.

The Hork-Bajir-Controllers roughly hauled him to his feet and shoved him toward the cages.

"Why couldn't you kill me?" the man shouted. "Why couldn't you just kill me?"

I knew why they hadn't killed him. They hadn't wanted to destroy a good host body.

I reached into my pocket and slid open the Ziploc bag all the way. I guided Illim up the sleeve of my jacket. I would stick my hands into the pool when I lowered myself down. That way he could wriggle free and be ready to reenter Mr. Tidwell.

The Hork-Bajir-Controllers at the edge of the pier signaled me forward.

It was my turn.

CHAPTER 21

I could feel my knees shaking as I knelt down at the edge of the pier. I took a deep breath and lowered my head into the sludge.

The first thing I did was release Illim. Then I slithered over to Mr. Tidwell's ear canal, breaking my connections to his brain. I scrunched my body down as I wiggled my way through the tiny tunnel.

Then I was free. Out in the Yeerk pool.

I was blind, almost deaf, and mute. But here's the strange part. I didn't care. I was with my brothers and sisters, soaking in the Kandrona rays my body craved. If I'd had a mouth, I would have let out a long ahhh of satisfaction. I was home.

I was *home*?

I gave myself a mental slap on both cheeks. I'd let my Yeerk instincts take over for a minute. This was definitely not home.

And I had a mission to complete. I had to find Aftran. Fast.

I used my sonar to check out the area around me. There were Yeerks everywhere. Above me. Below me. On all four sides.

I reminded myself that to them I was just another Yeerk. Nothing for them to take notice of. I was completely safe.

A Hork-Bajir head was thrust into the water. I rode the wave it created deeper into the pool. I did another sonar sweep. Yeerks, Yeerks, and more Yeerks.

A wavelet took me in a half turn. My sonar detected the two steel piers. Under the farthest one there was a chain with a box on the end. The box was just about the size to hold a Yeerk.

Aftran. She was in there. I knew it.

But how was I going to get over to her? I had no legs to kick with. No arms to paddle with.

I wiggled my body as hard as I could and moved about a quarter of an inch. Aftran was only about six feet away. But at this rate it would take me all night to get to her.

And I definitely didn't have all night.

Use the Yeerk, I told myself. *It knows how to swim.* I loosened my control over the Yeerk instincts.

Scrunch-thrust. Scrunch-thrust. Scrunch-thrust.

I contracted my body, then shot it out. I was swimming!

Well, sort of. I wasn't exactly ready for the Olympic team, but I was moving faster than I had been.

Scrunch-thrust. Scrunch-thrust. Scrunch-thrust.

I finally made it over to the cage. I studied it with my sonar. It was a box, metal I figured, with very small holes all over it. The holes were way too small for even a Yeerk to squeeze through.

But the latch looked pretty basic. It wouldn't be too hard to open. If I had hands.

I could demorph to my own body. But I was right under the pier. Two Hork-Bajir stood on the edge. And more walked back and forth, escorting the hosts. There was a pretty good chance one of them would notice me.

PA-loosh!

A host head was thrust into the water. My sonar picked up the wild movement as the host — an older man this time — tried to twist away from the Yeerk scrunch-thrusting toward his ear.

The Yeerk shoved its way inside the host, and moments later the man stopped struggling and calmly raised his head.

The hosts getting reinfested upped my chances of getting caught. A Yeerk could slither into its host, see me in my human morph, lift up its head, and report me.

I couldn't risk morphing so close to the pier. I had to find another way to get Aftran out.

PA-loosh.

Another host head was shoved into the pool. A girl. My sonar picked up her long hair flowing through the water. It was hard to tell, but I didn't think she was that much older than I was.

<I am ready to interrogate the prisoner.>

That voice. It was the voice of evil. It ripped through me, sending spikes of terror though my small, soft body.

Visser Three! He was back!

And I hadn't even found a way to open Aftran's cage!

<Bring Aftran Nine Four Two to me,> Visser Three commanded.

Aftran's cage immediately began to move through the pool. Someone was pulling the chain up. Pulling Aftran away from me.

And I had no hands to stop it.

But I had to do something. Now!

<Everyone is invited to the infestation pier,> Visser Three said, sounding jovial. <You are invited to witness the fate of traitors!>

CHAPTER 22

No time to plan. No time to do anything but move.

Scrunch-thrust. Scrunch-thrust. Scrunch-thrust.

I powered over to the girl whose head was in the water. A Yeerk was just about to enter her ear. I shoved it out of the way and slithered in myself.

I gave a squirt of painkiller and wriggled through the ear canal. I spread myself out over the brain. The microvolts of electricity set my body tingling. And I was connected.

I frantically opened the girl's memories. She was a member of The Sharing.

This girl — she was a voluntary host. A collaborator.

I couldn't let her get anything from me. No thoughts. No emotions. Nothing even the tiniest bit Cassie.

I felt hands on my shoulders, helping me out of the water. I stumbled to my feet.

Any second the girl was going to realize I wasn't her usual Yeerk. But she wouldn't be able to do anything to betray me. Not now. I had control of the body.

But as soon as I left her, she would be able to tell Visser Three everything she learned while I was in her head.

I had to act! Now! Before I let it slip that the Visser's "Andalite bandits" were mostly human. Before I betrayed Illim and Tidwell. Or the Chee.

I turned around and locked my eyes on Visser Three. In his Andalite morph. He stood halfway down the pier, facing away from me. A crowd of human- and Hork-Bajir-Controllers, and Taxxons gathered in front of him, eager to watch the torture.

The Visser unlatched Aftran's cage. Pulled her out. He held her up, digging his fingers into her defenseless flesh.

<You will tell me everything about the so-called peace movement,> Visser Three told Aftran, blasting his thought-speak loud enough for everyone to hear. <Then I'll have to use my imag-

ination and come up with a nice, long, painful way for you to die.>

Wham! Wham! Wham!

My feet slammed against the metal pier as I launched myself at him. The only thing my host girl was going to get from me was commands like <Run. Now. Fast. Go.>

I rammed into Visser Three as hard as I could.

He spun toward me, tail blade raised. But he was too shocked and amazed to react.

I snatched at Aftran.

The Visser closed his fist. But Andalite hands are weak.

I bit his wrist.

Aftran dropped. I snatched her out of midair and ran. Ran with nowhere to run.

I did the only thing I could do. I dove back into the Yeerk pool.

<Get her! Get them both! Bring them to me!> Visser Three roared. <Get them or I will fill this cavern with your dead bodies!>

PA-loosh. PA-loosh.

I took a quick glance over my shoulder. Taxxons. Two of them. You wouldn't think creatures that look like twelve-foot-long, four-foot-wide centipedes could swim. But they can.

And they were coming after me.

Aftran slipped out of my fingers. I hoped she knew to stay close to me.

TSEEEWWWW! TSEEEWWWW! TSEEEWWWW!

Spears of light streaked through the water. Great. Someone was shooting Dracon beams at me from the pier.

I propelled myself deeper into the water. The beams might still be able to reach me down here, but the shooter wouldn't be able to see me to aim.

TSEEEEEEW!

I saw a dozen Yeerks twist and burn.

The Visser was killing his own people to get at me.

I felt a claw pinch my ankle. A Taxxon, out of nowhere! It had me with one of its lobster hands.

Time to bail.

I pulled myself away from the girl's brain, squirmed through her ear canal, then slid into the pool.

With my sonar I watched the girl being dragged to the surface. It wouldn't take them long to figure out that the Yeerk who had been controlling her was no longer in her body.

I didn't doubt Visser Three would find a way to search the pool for me and Aftran.

I needed to get out of here. Now. Something with wings. I wanted wings in the worst kind of way.

But before I could morph to bird, I had to demorph into my human body. In the Yeerk pool.

I dove deep. Down below most of the other Yeerks. And I began to become human again.

My Yeerk body flattened out. Stretching, stretching, stretching. It formed a head. Arms. Legs. But all flat. I was like a giant paper doll.

I felt my bones regrow, pushing against my flat body. Making it three-dimensional again. My skin changed in texture, and I could no longer breathe through it.

Eyes, nose, lips pushed out of my paper-doll face.

A pounding started up in my chest as my heart re-formed. My veins and arteries expanded, and blood began to rush through them. My stomach and intestines plumped up inside me. My lungs inflated. And started to burn.

I needed air. Badly.

I paddled up to the top of the pool. I tilted my head back and allowed only my nose to break through the surface.

I pulled breath after breath into my aching lungs.

Then I heard the words that turned my body to stone.

<No one touch her,> Visser Three ordered. <I want the pleasure of killing her myself. After I find out everything that's in her pitiful excuse for a mind.>

CHAPTER 23

I swam. I swam hard. Then . . .

<This creature has no Yeerk!> the Visser cried.

He wasn't talking to me! He was talking to the girl whose body I'd used to attack him.

Any second now he would figure it out. Any second now . . .

<A second traitor! Some Yeerk used this host to . . . No! The Andalites! They're here!>

I took another long breath. Then pushed myself deeper into the pool. The Yeerks brushed against my arms, my legs, my face. The feel of their jellyfish-soft bodies repulsed me. I flicked them away. As fast as I did, new ones took their place.

Ignore them, I ordered myself. Now was not the time to get distracted. I needed to morph.

Morphing underwater without breathing was beyond risky. It was stupid. But I had to get out of the pool and I didn't have any backup. I had to take the chance.

An owl. It would be strong enough to carry Aftran. And its eyes would allow it to maneuver in the dim cavern.

I concentrated on the owl DNA inside me. I felt the feathers begin to form. They clung to my human body, wet and heavy. I would never be able to lift myself into the air with these drenched feathers! Forget about me and Aftran.

My lungs burned. But I couldn't risk another breath.

I ran through my other possible morphs. Which would give me the best chance to escape? Think, think, think! Shark. No. Dolphin. No. Squirrel. Maybe. No. My insect morphs were definitely out of the question.

I was starting to get dizzy. I was running out of time.

Wait. Got it! My osprey morph! Osprey hunted fish. That meant they had to be able to get wet and still fly!

I concentrated on the osprey DNA. I ignored the pressure building in my chest.

My legs grew thin. As thin as noodles. They swayed in the water for a moment before they began to shorten.

I felt my lips and nose melt together to form a beak. I choked as a mouthful of Yeerk pool sludge sloshed down my throat. The taste was bitter on my shrinking tongue.

Where were my wings? I needed wings!

My lungs throbbed. I couldn't hold my breath —

A pulling sensation raced up and down my arms as they stretched into wings. Yes!

<Aftran, get between my talons. Now! Hurry!> I cried though I knew she couldn't hear or answer.

I felt pinpricks cover my body as my feathers started to pop out. Aftran slid between my talons. I had her. At least I hoped it was her. We were out of there!

Red dots exploded in front of my eyes as I struggled to the surface. I pushed my beak through the surface and dragged in as much air as my lungs would hold.

<Okay, it's time for takeoff,> I told Aftran.

I powered my wings through the sludge, pushing my body up out of the Yeerk pool. I knew they'd be waiting for me. There was no way to sneak out.

"Visser! A bird!"

<Shoot it, you imbecile! It must not fly!>

TSEEEWWW! A Dracon beam fired at me. Missed.

I gave another hard flap, skimming across the surface of the pool, talons dragging. Almost airborne. Almost!

Zap!

A long yellow tentacle snaked out of the sludge and snapped me on the wing. The spot it hit instantly turned numb. Off balance, I tilted.

Sploosh! Half my body slipped down into the pool again.

The Visser! He had morphed to . . . to something that could swim. Something strong and fast.

<Going somewhere, my noble Andalite warrior?> Visser Three asked.

This time he was talking to me. Definitely.

And I was on my own. I didn't have Marco, Jake, Tobias, Rachel, or Ax to distract the Visser.

His new morph was terrifying. It was like a floating eyeball with long, long tentacles for lashes. One of those tentacles shot out and snapped me on the wing again. Numb.

His tentacles were filled with poison. If I got hit too many more times I wouldn't be able to move my wing at all. I'd sink straight to the bottom and the Visser —

Zap!

I took another hit. The opposite wing.

I had to get myself back out of the water.

I slammed my wings through the sludge.

Zap!

My bad wing again. It was almost half numb now.

Think of Ax. Think of Jake. I thrust my wings down again and again.

Rachel. Tobias. Marco.

More red dots exploding. I couldn't hold my breath much longer. I broke through the surface of the water.

Mom. Dad.

I pulled up, up, up. Muscles screaming in pain.

Yes! I was out of reach of the tentacles.

I wheeled around and flapped toward the staircase.

The humans in the cages cheered. The human-Controllers cursed and howled in fury. The Taxxons shrieked. The Hork-Bajir-Controllers bellowed.

I caught a glimpse of Mr. Tidwell. He pumped his fist in the air. To the others it probably looked like an angry gesture. But I knew it was triumph.

TSEEEWWWW! TSEEEWWWW! TSEEEWWWW!

I zigzagged as well as I could with my injured wings, Aftran still clutched in my talons.

Hork-Bajir-Controllers fired at me from the pier.

<Would it be asking too much for one of you to actually hit something?!!> I heard Visser Three roar.

I reached the stairs. Up, up, up I flew. Gulping for air. Lungs on fire.

The rock walls changed to dirt. The Dracon beams fired from the pier couldn't reach me here.

<Almost out, Aftran!> I cried. I pumped harder. Couldn't slow down. Not now!

TSEEEWWWWW!

A sharp, acrid scent flooded me. The smell of my own feathers. The Dracon beam had singed them.

I made a sharp turn to the left. Now I saw what I had missed in my frenzy.

It floated through the air, heading for me. A seemingly weightless metallic ball.

A hunter robot.

CHAPTER 24

I knew the hunter robot only had one weak spot. Its visual aiming system.

I flapped hard, struggling to get some altitude. I moved into position above the hunter robot.

I only had one chance. I waited for it.

The big metal ball rotated until its camera lens was pointed up at me. In one second it would fire.

BLAT!

A gray-white blob fell.

My life, Aftran's life, the life of all my friends, the future of the human race, hung on that falling blob.

It hit the lens.

The robot spun to the right. Then to the left. Then to the right again.

A bird-poop bull's-eye.

I beat wings up to the metal door. There was no handle on my side. Only smooth, shiny metal.

I scanned the wall around the door. There had to be some kind of trigger mechanism, didn't there?

Maybe it's only an entrance, I thought. Maybe it's like the changing room at the Gap. People enter the Yeerk pool there. But they go out through the movie theater.

I swooped a little closer.

BrrrrEEEEET! BrrrrEEEEET!

Oh, no! The Gleet BioFilter.

I'd forgotten all about it. How could I have been so stupid?

"Unauthorized life-form detected," a mechanical voice announced. BrrrrEEEEET! Brrrr-EEEEET! "Unauthorized life-form detected."

In seconds I would be destroyed. The BioFilter eliminated all life-forms whose DNA had not been entered in the computer. Ospreys were definitely not on the Yeerks' invite list.

Could I morph to Yeerk in time? Would my human morph be better?

I heard the sound of feet pounding up the stairs toward me. Really big feet. Hork-Bajir warriors.

"Shut your eyes tightly to protect against retinal damage from the Gleet BioFilter," the mechanical voice instructed.

I was doomed.

Whoosh!

The metal door split down the middle. A woman started through. She spotted me.

"Andalite!" she cried. She swiped at me with her purse. I banked hard, ignoring the pain tearing through my damaged wing.

A purse wasn't enough to stop me. Not nearly enough.

I flew into the cold air of the walk-in freezer. The outside door was swinging shut. Could I make it?

The room exploded in dazzling white light.

Clang! I bounced off one of the metal shelves.

Crash! Something that sounded like falling glass.

I didn't stop. I flew straight ahead.

Made it! Thump! The freezer door shut behind me.

I lost a couple of tail feathers, but I kept flying.

"Dad, look, a bird!" I heard a little girl yell.

"What is that thing it's carrying?" someone else cried.

A little of my vision was coming back. Enough that I could just make out the front door.

Of course it was shut. You don't realize how much you need your hands until you don't have them.

But you know what's cool? Humans. Nine out of ten humans are pretty decent creatures.

One of those nice humans, concerned for a bird obviously panicked by being trapped, opened the door.

I blew through.

I flew, flew, flew into free, wide-open skies.

<As Marco would say if he were here: That was interesting. Let's never, *ever* do it again.>

I was relieved. But I didn't have time to celebrate. I had to get home. Ax needed me.

I flew like mad for home. My body was trembling with exhaustion when I finally sailed in the hayloft window. I landed on a bale of hay and released Aftran.

<I'll get you in some water in a minute,> I promised her.

My little bird heart was pounding like crazy. I wanted to fluff up my feathers and stick my head under my wing. Instead, I concentrated on my own DNA.

The feathers covering my body flattened until they were two-dimensional tattoos. My hollow bones grew and solidified. I heard a sloshing sound as my internal organs shifted and changed.

My bird eyes grew, and my vision became

completely clear again. I watched the last few changes. Then I shoved myself up with a grunt. I scooped up Aftran and headed to Ax's stall.

I couldn't stop myself from gasping when I opened the door and stepped through the hologram. Ax was lying on his side. He never does that. And I could hear him breathing in short, ragged pants.

"He's in crisis," Erek told me.

CHAPTER 25

I knelt next to Ax. "I'm back," I told him. "I'm right here with you."

He didn't answer.

"He's unconscious," Erek told me. "Has been for a little more than half an hour."

"Poor baby." I ran my fingers over his soft blue-and-tan fur. His sides heaved with every breath he took.

"I don't think you have much time," Erek said gently.

"You're right." I stood up and slid Aftran into the water trough.

"You'll be safe there," I told her. I knew she couldn't understand me. I knew she had to be terrified. But I had to leave her.

I turned to Erek. "I'm worried about hurting him when we move him. Maybe we could —"

Erek bent down and scooped Ax up in his arms. I'd forgotten for a minute how amazingly strong the Chee are.

I leaned over the stall door and checked to make sure the barn was still empty. Then I opened the door and led the way to the operating room. I pointed to the metal table and Erek placed Ax on top.

"Can you do another hologram to make the room look empty?" I asked. "Just in case."

"You got it," Erek answered.

I couldn't believe I was doing this. I couldn't believe I was actually going to perform brain surgery. On an alien.

I suddenly had this powerful urge to walk away. To go find a TV, plant myself in front of it with a pint of Ben and Jerry's, crank the volume, and forget everything.

"Probably nothing on, anyway," I muttered.

"What?"

"Nothing."

Just take it one step at a time, I coached myself. But what should the first step be? I closed my eyes and tried to picture what my dad did before an operation and what I'd seen in the books I'd gotten from my mom. Got it. Step one: Get things clean. Duh.

Numbly I walked over to the sink and washed my hands with antibacterial soap. I dried them, then pulled on a pair of latex gloves.

I took a bottle of rubbing alcohol off the shelf and grabbed a jar of cotton balls. I soaked one of the balls.

"This will feel a little cold," I told Ax before I started swabbing his head. I knew he couldn't hear me. But it made me feel a little better to talk to him.

I tossed the used cotton ball in the garbage and carefully returned the alcohol and the rest of the cotton balls to their proper places. I was stalling. And that could be deadly to Ax. I didn't know how much time he had left.

I jerked open the long drawer in the middle of my dad's cabinet and pulled out a scalpel. I took it over to Ax. My heart was thudding so loud I could feel it all over my body. In my ears. Even in my fingertips.

I positioned the scalpel over Ax's head. Then I froze. How could I just make a cut? Where was the *Tria* gland?!

Maybe I could feel it through Ax's scalp. Maybe there would be swelling. Or a spot that felt hotter or colder.

I used my free hand to examine Ax's head. I started with his forehead. Nothing. I moved up to the space between his eye stalks. Nothing. I checked the area around each of his ears. Nothing. I ran my fingers over every inch of the back of his skull, twice. Nothing. Nothing.

"This is hopeless! It's impossible!" I cried. "He's going to die with me standing right next to him!"

"You've already done one hopeless, impossible thing tonight," Erek reminded me.

Rescuing Aftran from Visser Three had felt pretty impossible. Pretty hopeless. Now Aftran was safe and sound —

Wait.

Wait.

My mind seemed to slow down and speed up at the same time.

Aftran!

"Be right back," I told Erek. I dashed out of the operating room and over to Ax's stall. I scooped Aftran out of the trough and raced back.

I skidded to a stop at the edge of the operating room table. I brought Aftran up to one of Ax's ears. Her Yeerk instincts should tell her to go inside.

Yes! Aftran slithered across my palm and into the opening of Ax's ear canal. I watched as her slick gray body disappeared inside.

"Maybe she'll be able to tell us where the *Tria* gland is," I told Erek. I gripped the metal table with both hands.

"You're brilliant," Erek said. "Unless . . ."

"Yeah. Let's wait and see if it works first," I answered.

I stared down at Ax. Waiting.

Aftran should be pushing herself into Ax's brain right now, I thought. Once she's in control, she'd be able to talk. Wouldn't she?

This had to work. It had to. If it didn't —

Don't, I ordered myself. *Aftran will come through.*

But why wasn't she saying anything? Why was this taking so long? Was she having trouble with the Andalite brain? Was Ax's illness making it impossible for her to connect?

<Cassie?> Aftran said in Andalite thought-speak.

"I'm here. We got away from Visser Three. You're inside my friend, Ax," I explained, talking as fast as I could. "There's a gland in his head that's going to explode any second. If it does, he dies. I have to take it out, but I don't know where it is. Can you feel it? Can you tell me where to cut?"

<The *Tria* gland. Yes, I have accessed his memories,> she answered. <It is . . . it is unusual to attempt this. I have few nerve endings . . . no way to feel what . . . wait!>

"What?" Erek demanded. "Wait what?"

<Got it! But, Cassie, it feels very warm.>

I grabbed a scalpel with trembling fingers. "Just tell me where to cut."

CHAPTER 26

< The *Tria* gland is in the back of the head,> Aftran explained. <It's even with the bottom of his ears. Dead center.>

I turned Ax's head so I could easily reach that spot. "Okay, I'm going to make the first incision," I told her. "Stay out of the way."

<The gland is about as big as a human thumb. Well, Karen's thumb, at least.>

"Thanks." I picked up the scalpel and positioned it to one side of the spot Aftran had described. Then I made a straight cut about four inches long. I could feel the metal blade scraping the bone of Ax's skull.

But that was good. That's how deep I needed

to go. I needed to peel back a flap of skin so I could work on the bone.

A line of blue-black blood appeared. My stomach did a flip-flop. I swallowed hard and made a cut that was perpendicular to the first, again about four inches long.

"Hemostat!" I snapped.

The instrument was in my hand a split second later.

"Another. Okay. Retractor. No, it's that other thing!"

I pulled back a flap of skin.

"Tape," I said.

"How much do you want?" Erek asked.

"Three inches."

He passed the piece of cloth tape to me. I used it to hold the flap of skin away from the bone.

<His hearts are starting to beat faster. And the gland is still throbbing. It's swelled a little, too,> Aftran announced.

"Can you control his heartbeats at all?" I asked. "Try to slow them down?"

<I'll try,> she said.

"Gauze pads, Erek." I held out my hand and Erek slapped them in my hand. I used them to mop up some of the blood oozing out of the incision.

"Now the hole saw. It's in the sterilizer."

"Here."

<You need to hurry, Cassie,> Aftran said. <It doesn't look good in here.>

Aftran sounded nervous. What would happen to her if Ax's *Tria* gland burst while she was still inside his head?

"Okay, I'm going to need you to blot some of the blood away as I go," I told Erek.

"You got it."

Erek handed me the hole saw. I positioned the circle of saw teeth around where I hoped the *Tria* gland was. I turned the saw's handle a few times.

I pulled the saw back, and the circle of bone came with it. Now I was looking at Ax's brain.

Sweat popped out all over my forehead and started to run down my cheeks and nose. Erek dabbed it away with another gauze pad before it could start dripping onto Ax's brain.

I didn't have to ask Aftran for more help finding the *Tria* gland. It was easy to spot. Deep purple. Bulging.

"Retractor," I told Erek. "Scalpel."

My fingers shook when he handed them to me. The gland looked ready to blow. I was afraid if I touched it, it would start spewing.

"Hold this. My left eye! Sweat!"

He swabbed my eye with a cotton ball.

"Okay. Let's do it," I whispered.

141

I slid the scalpel blade beneath the gland with trembling care.

I cut.

The *Tria* gland was out. I tossed it into a metal pan.

"Okay." I wrapped my arms around myself. My whole body was shaking.

Don't lose it now, I thought.

As quickly as I could, I replaced the circle of bone. It would fuse back in place in time. I untaped the flap of skin and smoothed it down.

"Now we sew."

<His heart rates are slowing down. His blood pressure is going down, too,> Aftran reported.

"That was one of the coolest things I've ever seen," Erek said with a laugh. "And I've seen a lot."

<Cassie, he's coming to,> Aftran announced. <And he's starting to scream!>

CHAPTER 27

"What's wrong?" I cried. "Am I hurting him?"

<No,> Aftran said, her voice suddenly flat. <He's screaming because there's a Yeerk in his head.>

"Ax, listen to me. The Yeerk is Aftran. She helped me save your life," I cried.

<He's totally freaking,> Aftran told me. <He's saying you should have let him die. He would have killed himself with his own blade before he let a Yeerk infest him.>

"He doesn't understand," I answered.

<Yes, he does,> she insisted. <I'm coming out.>

A moment later, Aftran slithered out of Ax's ear.

143

Ax bucked on the table. His eye stalks jerked back and forth. <Where is it?> he cried. <Don't let it touch me!>

I grabbed his head between my hands. "Stop it!" I ordered angrily. "You have to stay still until I finish stitching your head!"

Ax obediently lay back on the table, but I could see tremors running through his body. My anger faded. Ax had been so sick. Then he'd come to and found a Yeerk in his head. One of the monsters who had killed his brother.

No wonder he went off. He probably thought he'd been captured and infested.

"You're okay," I told Ax soothingly. "You're in my dad's operating room. I put Aftran in your head. She looked inside you and told me where the *Tria* gland was. She helped me operate. I got it out. You're past your crisis."

I scooped up Aftran, filled the sink with water, and let her inside. "I'll be back in a minute," I promised her. Even though she was deaf again. Blind, mute. Helpless.

I turned back to Ax. He kept rubbing his ear. I knew he was feeling violated. Repulsed by what I had done to him.

"Visser Three was planning to interrogate Aftran tonight," I said softly as I returned to stitching up Ax's incision. "He discovered she was part of the peace movement."

<Filthy Yeerk,> he spat.

I made the last stitch. "That filthy Yeerk helped save your life. And she very nearly gave her life for peace between human and Yeerk. And now, unless I can think of some way to save her, she will die a slow death of Kandrona starvation."

Ax didn't say anything. Maybe when he'd gotten some rest, he'd think it over.

"Erek, would you take Ax back to the stall?" I asked. "He'll need at least a few days to recover. Is that too long for you to stay and keep the hologram up?"

Erek gently lifted Ax off the table. "You're talking to a guy who helped build the pyramids. A few days is nothing."

I smiled at him. "Thanks. I couldn't have gotten through all this without you."

"Yes, you could have. But you're welcome," he answered as he carried Ax out the door.

I sat down on the little stool my dad keeps by the table. I wrapped my arms around my knees. All the fear I'd been pushing away suddenly hit me. I felt like my body was deflating.

It's just a delayed reaction, I told myself. You're safe. Ax is safe. Aftran's safe.

That wasn't really true. Yeah, I got Aftran away from Visser Three. But in three days, she would be dead.

I pushed myself to my feet and leaned against the sink, staring down at her. She had done what few have the strength to do. She had questioned the beliefs she had been raised with. And ultimately, she had chosen to go against her society. To turn away from everything she had once believed, to become the enemy of those closest to her.

Aftran had sacrificed so much. She had experienced all the richness and wonder of our world. But when she decided she did not have the right to control another, she had been strong enough to give it up to save a little girl's life.

She returned to the Yeerk pool. It must have felt like the worst kind of prison to her after being in Karen's body. But she didn't allow herself to wallow in despair. She chose to fight. She battled to free us all.

I reached into the water and slid Aftran into my hands. I pressed her against my ear. It was the only way I could talk to her, and I needed to thank her for all she'd done.

A moment later I felt her cold, slick body touch my skin. My ear canal tingled as she pushed her way through.

<I knew you would come for me, Cassie,> she said as soon as she had made her connections with my brain.

There was so much I wanted to say to her, I

hardly knew where to start. <Thank you for helping me save Ax's life,> I answered.

She laughed. <If you had told me when we first met that I would ever do anything to aid an Andalite . . .>

<Or become a Yeerk freedom fighter,> I added.

<That, too,> Aftran agreed. Her tone turned somber then. <Cassie, there's something I have to ask you to do for me.>

<Anything,> I replied instantly.

<I need you to kill me,> she said simply.

<What?> I cried. <No!>

<We both know I will be dead in three days no matter what you do. You have witnessed Kandrona starvation. I ask you to spare me that,> Aftran answered. <End my life now. You can make it fast and painless.>

I felt a lump of unshed tears form in my throat. Were they mine? Or Aftran's?

Maybe they were both of ours.

Both of ours. That gave me an idea.

<You could stay in me!> I exclaimed.

<No. You would have to go into the Yeerk pool every three days. It's too dangerous. If you were somehow found out, Visser Three would learn everything about your friends and the peace movement. All would be lost,> Aftran answered.

She must have felt the wave of despair and sorrow sweeping through me.

<It's not so bad to die for what you believe in. There are much worse deaths,> she said gently. <Many worse deaths.>

CHAPTER 28

"My mom didn't let me eat any solid food until today," Rachel complained. "And it's been four days since I got sick."

All the way to the beach, Jake, Rachel, Marco, Tobias, and Ax had been trying to top each other with stories about who felt worse when they were sick.

<That's the worst thing that happened to you while you were sick?> Tobias demanded as he soared overhead. <I'm not even sure Cassie's dad is a real vet. He tried to stick a pill up —>

"Yeah, well, my dad brought me baby aspirin from the store. Baby aspirin!" Marco groused. "Like for a baby."

"A Yeerk was in my head," Ax said, still amazed. He was in human morph, naturally. "In my head. Head-duh."

I mostly ignored my friends' complaining contest. I was enjoying the warm sand sliding between my toes. And the salty smell and soft sounds of the ocean.

There's nothing like a trip to the Yeerk pool to make you appreciate life and freedom.

"Is this where we're supposed to meet Aftran?" Jake asked.

"Uh-huh. When I morphed to dolphin and visited her this morning, she said it's time for her to move on. But she wanted to say good-bye," I answered. "Just look out there." I pointed out at the blue-green water.

"I don't see anything," Marco said.

<I do,> Tobias answered. <Turn a little to the left.>

We turned. I scanned the ocean and spotted a foamy spot. The water broke over a massive fin.

Then a humpback whale leaped. All the way out of the water. Droplets of water flew off her in a sparking comet.

There should be a picture of that scene in the dictionary — under beauty. And joy.

"We made the right decision," Jake said. "Better than the last time we used the blue box."

"Would have been hard to do any worse," Marco said. "Anyway. Visser Three will never find Aftran now."

On Aftran's second day out of the Yeerk pool, everyone in the group was well enough for a short meeting. We all agreed that we couldn't let Aftran die. It was Jake who thought of the way to save her.

He suggested that we give her the power to morph, on the condition that she choose one morph and stay in it forever. It was just safer that way. For everyone. Like I said, the decision was unanimous.

Aftran took another sparking flight. I felt like my heart was leaping with her.

"Whoa! Good leap!" Marco exclaimed.

It felt good. We were all together again. Alive. Well. And Aftran was free. How amazing was that?

<Aftran's moving out. Heading for the deep ocean,> Tobias announced.

"She must feel like she's in paradise," I said. "Can you imagine living in the ocean after the Yeerk pool? And in that body — fast, powerful, able to see, hear, feel, and communicate."

"I bet she'll miss the fight though," Rachel added.

"She's done her part," Jake said.

151

I thought back to that moment when I had first allowed Aftran into my head. One decision, so many consequences.

I caught Jake watching me.

"What?" I asked.

He shrugged. "Just wondering what you were thinking."

"Nothing very profound," I said. "Just . . ."

"Just what?"

"Just that every now and then, we actually win one."

He nodded. "Sometimes we do win," he agreed. "This time? This time, Cassie, *you* won."

With a clean face and conditioned hair I headed toward the school bus stop.

And walked past it.

Instead, I hopped on a city bus headed downtown.

The warren of streets that is the financial and business center of our town seemed as good a place as any to kill time. To get lost without running the risk of running into anyone who knew me.

There were movie theaters downtown. I figured I'd look around till I could catch a matinee of something loud and fun.

Twenty minutes later the bus dropped me and thirty office-bound men and women in the heart of blue-suit central.

It was still way early but already the sun was heating up the sidewalks, and the exhaust from the cars, trucks, and buses was spread like a grubby, smelly blanket over the concrete and steel jungle.

Nice choice, Marco. I should have gone to the beach. I stood on the sidewalk and stared.

Seething mass of humanity. I'd heard that phrase once and now I knew what it meant. It meant "office workers at rush hour."

What was the big hurry? Did adults really like going to work? Or was Friday free donut day at the office?

THWACK!

I was down! My knees hit the pavement and my face landed in a planter full of cigarette butts and abandoned coffee cups.

The enemy! I prepared myself for the next blow.

Nothing. I looked up.

No one had noticed I'd been knocked over.

I got to my feet, dazed. I rubbed the ash, dirt, and stale coffee off my face with the bottom of my shirt.

I was disgusted. And I was mad.

A woman had run me over with her tank of a briefcase. Then she'd continued on down the street like nothing had happened. And no one had stopped to help me.

"And they say *my* generation has no manners," I muttered.

I gave myself a quick once-over — nothing

seriously damaged but my dignity — and set out after the woman who'd so callously whacked me. This woman had an appointment with the dirty pavement, courtesy of a well-placed Saucony Cross Trainer.

I caught up to her about halfway down the block and followed a few feet behind. Waiting for my chance. Her briefcase was big enough to hold a Doberman and built to maim, with steel corners and a big combination lock on the side.

And what was up with that hair? The woman wore a stiff, curly blond wig. Think steel wool pad. Used. Slightly shredded. And yellow.

I saw the perfect spot to exact my revenge.

I skirted the crowd and hid behind a big, concrete column about a yard ahead, just at the corner of the courthouse. When Wig Lady passed — bingo, bango! BAM!

She was going down.

I peeked from around the pillar to see how close she was to meeting my foot. And then I bit my cheek to stop from screaming.

The woman with the awful blond hair and the briefcase . . .

Was my mother!

Visser One!

Elfangor's Secret

"You mentioned a deal," Marco said.

"Yes," the Drode said. "A deal. And here it is: The six of you will be allowed to follow the Time Matrix. The former Visser Four set off on his journey two days ago. You will be translated back to that point and then the quanta that make up your atoms will be . . . tuned. Yes, that's a good word for simple minds to comprehend. You'll be fine-tuned at the subatomic level to resonate with the movements of the Time Matrix as it travels through time. Your own memories and personalities will, of course, be buffered. Protected against changes."

<Resulting in what effect?> Ax demanded.

"Resulting in the effect that, like an echo, you will follow the Time Matrix. It plucks the chords of time and you reverberate." He stopped and shook his head in admiration of his own words. "Brilliantly explained, eh?"

"That's the deal?" Jake asked. "That's it?"

"There's something else, isn't there?" I asked the Drode.

The Drode laughed. "Oh, yes. There is something else, little Cassie. Cassie the killer with a conscience. Kill 'em, then cry over 'em. That's our Cassie."

"What's the something else?" I repeated, not letting the evil little creep see that his words had hit home.

"My master Crayak has demanded a price. A payment."

"A payment."

"Uh-huh," the Drode said in a parody of coyness.

"What?"

"One of you," the Drode said. "You can attempt to save your reality, put everything back where it belongs, end slavery, replace tyranny with democracy, millions of lives saved, let freedom ring, glory hallelujah in exchange . . . in exchange for one, single life."

"A life?" I asked.

"The life of one of you. That is my master Crayak's price: One of you must die."

ANIMORPHS™

Collect your favorite Animorphs character action figures.

NEW!

Cassie morphs into a wolf.   Jake morphs into a bear

< MAKE THE CHANGE >

Also Available: Rachel/Lion Jake/Tiger Tobias/Hawk Marco/Gorilla

Invading Toy Stores Everywhere

SCHOLASTIC

Hasbro

Have you experienced the changes online?

Up-to-the-minute info
on the Animorphs!

Sneak previews
of books and
TV episodes!

Contests!

Fun downloads
and games!

Messages from
K.A. Applegate!

See what other fans
are saying on the Forum!

Check out the official Animorphs Web site at:
www.scholastic.com/animorphs

It'll change the way you see things.

There's a place that shouldn't exist,
but does...

Ever ∞ World
World

by K.A. Applegate

**A new series from
the author of Animorphs.**

Coming in June.